ST. GEORGE
AND
THE DRAGON

By

MICHAEL LOTTI

Illustrated by Jennifer Soriano

ISBN: 1496153545
ISBN 13: 9781496153548

Library of Congress Control Number: 2014904456
CreateSpace Independent Publishing Platform
North Charleston, South Carolina

For Tricia

TABLE OF CONTENTS

AUTHOR'S NOTE

This is a story of Saint George. I say *a* story and not *the* story, for no one knows much about Saint George.

We know that he lived somewhere in modern-day Turkey around 300 A.D. We know that he was a soldier in the Roman army. He was executed because he was a Christian, probably as a part of the persecutions begun by the Emperor Diocletian. All the stories of St. George say that he defeated a dragon.

The rest is unclear. Some stories say that he was raised as a Christian; others say that he converted to Christianity as an adult. Some stories say that he confronted the Emperor Diocletian directly; others report that he died in obscurity. Some stories tell of him performing miracles; others state that he simply defended the Christian faith.

I have taken what is known and what is guessed at and added many of my own guesses to create a story about a great Christian man. I have, of course, included a dragon. Many other stories about Saint George could be written. Perhaps you will write your own one day.

CHAPTER ONE

A LEAVE OF ABSENCE

The man rode steadily toward a tent in the distance. He was young and strong. He looked ahead with confidence, and he obviously enjoyed the speed of his horse, which was also young and strong. The horse's muscles rippled, and its all-white hide shone dully with sweat. The horse carried the man, a shield, a sword, a spear, and a large bundle. It ran hard, but its face was relaxed, not strained.

The man's name was Marcellus. Later, his name would be changed to "George," and he would look ahead with a different sort of confidence. But as he rode toward the tent, he did not know that. The horse's name was Kopto, the Greek word for "hammer."

Marcellus rode Kopto to the tent and was hailed by soldiers guarding it. Marcellus dismounted expertly, and many soldiers embraced him while others hurried to bring oats and water to Kopto.

"He is expecting you," said one of the soldiers, pointing to the tent. "We all know about your recent attack. Some have heard that he wants to promote you again."

Marcellus smiled but did not reply. He took a goblet of water offered by a soldier and drank it down. He splashed his face from a basin that another soldier held out to him.

"The only way he can promote me," responded Marcellus to the first soldier as he toweled off his face and hands, "is if he gives me his job. He will not do that, and I do not want him to."

"Yes, but someday, someday...," the soldier's voice trailed off in thought. "You know, sir, that we would fight for you like we fight for him."

Marcellus clapped the soldier's back. "I know. Someday, then!"

"Yes, sir! Someday!"

Marcellus straightened his uniform and confidently walked into the tent.

* * *

The tent was sparse, in the old Roman style. A banner with a double-headed eagle hung in one corner, and a bust of the Emperor Diocletian stood in another. Nothing else suggested that this was the tent of the highest ranking army officer in the region. There were no tables full of wine in silver goblets, no smells of rich foods or exotic spices, no conspicuously displayed letters from high-ranking officials in the empire.

Marcellus nodded. Demetrios is still a common soldier at heart, he thought. He knew that Demetrios disliked the younger officers who burdened their tents with luxuries and laced their banners with gold. He had heard that some of these young officers – especially those with a family connection to the emperor – even demanded that soldiers deliver reports while kneeling. He had also heard that these officers had a difficult time keeping order in camps and during campaigns. Some had resorted to using harsh punishments for even minor misbehavior.

Not so with Demetrios, thought Marcellus. His officers, his common soldiers, and even his slaves serve him out of respect,

"He looked ahead with confidence, and he obviously enjoyed the speed of his horse, which was also young and strong."

some even out of love. There was discipline, to be sure, but everyone knew that Demetrios' punishments came from his devotion to the empire and the army, not a falsely glorified image of himself.

Marcellus noticed a sack by his feet. When he moved his head, he could see a small mass of curled, yellowed papers in it.

Books, he thought. That is strange for Demetrios.

But before he could look further, Demetrios walked in and Marcellus lifted his arm in salute. Demetrios quickly saluted back and then embraced Marcellus. He laughed, and his laugh seemed to echo off every wall of the tent. Marcellus could not help smiling.

"My good Marcellus!" Demetrios shouted. He held Marcellus back and looked directly into Marcellus' eyes. "Good reports about you, Marcellus, always good. Your recent action against the Sassanids was magnificent. How many soldiers did you lose?"

"Ten, sir."

"And how many Sassanids were killed?"

"Dozens, sir. Perhaps a hundred."

"And you personally, Marcellus? I've heard reports that you went first into the enemy's camp. Not every tribune would have done that."

Marcellus flushed. "I thought to lead as you lead, sir."

Demetrios' laugh again filled the tent. "And who does old Demetrios imitate, eh?" He again laughed loudly. "Now do not be bashful, Marcellus. How many?"

Marcellus looked down and thought for a moment. "Twelve, sir. Maybe a few more. It was dark, and I may have only wounded some who died by another Roman hand."

"Twelve!" Demetrios shouted as he roughly placed his arm around Marcellus' neck. "A good number! A successful and important raid, too. Very important! The Sassanids won't be able to use that road for months now. They will be stuck on the other side of those hills, where they belong! Believe me, Marcellus, those who outrank me in the army have already noticed."

Demetrios lowered his voice, but his grip around Marcellus' neck did not yield. "This tent: it could be yours," he emphasized. "It *should* be yours. A few more raids, a few more years, and after that – the empire needs you, Marcellus."

Demetrios let go of Marcellus and assumed a slightly more detached tone as he turned away. "You must want something, Marcellus. What is it?"

Marcellus smiled at Demetrios' attempt to be formal. "I want to talk about my leave, sir."

Demetrios turned back, saw Marcellus smiling, and smiled himself. "Of course!" he boomed. "How long do you have?"

"Thirty days, sir, but –"

"But you want more. Let me guess: you want to get married."

Marcellus swallowed hard. How did Demetrios know? And what would he say? Marcellus knew that Roman soldiers had orders to never get married, but he also knew that this rule was regularly ignored. Half of his own soldiers had families. Word had spread, however, that some of the new officers were enforcing the rule with loss of pay and even expulsion from the army.

Demetrios clasped Marcellus around the neck again and looked into his eyes. "Don't worry!" he laughed. "You've noticed, I'm sure, that married soldiers work harder than the others?"

Marcellus realized that this was true. "Yes, sir, they do. But why?"

"Because they have something to fight for, of course! Will the common farm boy die for the great empire? No. But he will die for his children's empire, so that they speak Latin and not Sassanid or barbaric German. Even slaves with families are better workers."

"Yes, sir. I suppose that's true."

"I almost married, you know. My parents had it all arranged. But I chose the empire. Someone like you can fight for both, though." He walked back to the other side of the tent. "You need longer than 30 days? Fine. Forty days then – even a few more if you need them. I'll have new orders for you when you return. Cargalla will be in charge of your men while you are gone?"

"Yes, sir."

"Good. He's another soldier like you. Where will you be going?"

"To my father's estate in Galatia."

Demetrios' laugh echoed again. "Dragon country!" He continued laughing, but noticed that Marcellus was too puzzled to smile. "Just another folk tale, my dear Marcellus. A dragon flies around the Galatian countryside and eats cows in a single bite! And two weeks ago, I heard about a shark the size of a trireme off the coast of Greece! And from the north, barbarians bigger than tall trees!"

Demetrios clapped his hands twice while continuing to laugh. A small man with dark skin came in hurriedly, looking down. The man got orders to record Marcellus' leave and left as quickly as he came, looking down the whole time.

A wretched slave from one of Demetrios' expeditions, Marcellus thought. He shuddered as he remembered the time he had almost been captured by a Persian soldier.

"You can be on your way, Marcellus. A good trip to you, and a happy wedding!"

"Thank you, sir. Before I leave, tell me why these books are here. You are not much of a reader, are you?"

Demetrios' laugh bellowed again, but his face darkened. "That's the great and glorious empire at work! Actually, a waste of time and soldiers. Those are Christian books taken from Christian soldiers. Orders from the emperor himself, but everyone knows that Galerius is behind it. Cost me a good soldier, too."

"Why?"

"One of these Christians would not give up his book. He would not even let me hold it while he came to read it at night. I tried everything, Marcellus: the empire, the glory of the ancient gods, his ability to worship the Christian god in private. Nothing! Had to cut his head off in the end."

Marcellus frowned. In his eight years in the army, the number of Christian soldiers had grown. Rooting them out would not be easy or wise, he thought. The Christians under his command were all good soldiers. He had noticed that they refrained from the riotous feasts and gambling that ruined the lives of other promising soldiers.

"Do you think this policy will continue, sir?" asked Marcellus.

"I hope not, but do not underestimate Galerius. He loves power and hates Christians. It will certainly get worse before it gets better." Demetrios paused and looked away. "You have not become a Christian, have you, Marcellus?"

Marcellus was surprised. "No, sir. I confess that I read one of their books. It was about the life of Jesus. One of my officers got a fever and gave it to me right before he died."

Demetrios turned around and slowly eyed Marcellus. "And what did you think?"

"It was very strange, sir. Nothing like other histories I have read. And this Jesus was not nearly as sophisticated as philosophers like Seneca and Cicero." Marcellus paused. "He was a compelling figure, maybe even a great man. But he seemed so young and naïve."

Demetrios' eyes brightened as his laughter bellowed yet again. "That is it, that is it! He was well-meaning but foolish. And in the end a traitor too, to the empire and to his own people. Maybe Galerius is right: the Christians are not as harmless as they seem. Do not get involved with them, Marcellus. And look out for those Platonists too!" He laughed loudly again. "Cicero's the man for me. No nonsense!"

Marcellus smiled. "My father has every book by Cicero in his library. He quotes Cicero in every letter he sends."

"He is a good man, your father. Many still talk about his great leadership. 'If only Titus were still the commander,' they say. The best commanders are always the ones who have retired!" Demetrios put his arm around Marcellus' neck again and led him out of the tent. "Forty days, my good Marcellus. Plenty of time for you to read Cicero, too. Maybe you can read some to your wife!" He laughed again.

Kopto whinnied and stomped at the sight of Marcellus. Demetrios stroked Kopto's neck admiringly as Marcellus mounted. Marcellus saluted.

"Greet your father, Titus, for me! And look out for dragons!" Demetrios yelled with another laugh as Marcellus rode away.

CHAPTER TWO

BANDITS

Habitually alert to danger, Marcellus noticed the smoke as it appeared over the horizon.

As Marcellus drew closer, he made sure his sword unsheathed easily, and he readied his spear and shield. He also took out a gold coin from his money pouch. Before they saw him, he had counted six men and ten horses in the camp. "Bandits," he growled. Under his breath, he cursed the recent emperors who, in their greed and lust for power, had allowed such nomadic criminals to flourish.

He assessed the physical situation. The camp was on the right side of the road, down a small embankment. A large fire burned at the center of it. To the left of the road was a thickly wooded, steep ridge.

Perfect, Marcellus thought.

When the men at the campsite noticed him, they shouted and scrambled to mount horses. Marcellus was not surprised to see them stumble and sway as much as they did. He had observed that most criminals and barbarians – and even a few soldiers – drank wine all day.

He advanced until he was a spear's throw away from the bandits. He held up his hands and shouted, "I am Marcellus, tribune in the army of the Empire. I am traveling to my father's home and wish to pass in peace."

The men talked among themselves. Marcellus could not hear them very well, but he was sure that he heard the words "gold" and "easy" more than once. Three of the men advanced together on their horses while the other three went down the embankment into their camp. Once in the camp, one of the men took up a bow and arrow.

Marcellus waited until the three advancing men were at the narrowest part of the road before he moved forward. As he expected, they stopped as soon as he moved. Their horses were thin and ragged, and the men mirrored them. Marcellus guessed that he would be able to smell them if the wind had been blowing in his direction.

Marcellus held up his hand again, this time with the gold coin visible in it. "I wish to pass in peace and I am willing to pay you for that."

There was a pause, then coarse laughter. "I told you he had gold," shouted one.

Marcellus did not wait. He buried the coin in his purse, grasped the shield with his right hand and the spear with his left. He charged directly at the bandit farthest on his right, cutting off any retreat into the camp. Startled, the man tried to move to his right, but the other two bandits, blocked by the ridge, were in his way. Before the bandit could face Marcellus, the spear went into his chest and he toppled off his horse. The horse reared in panic, causing the other two horses to rear as well. One of the riders fell to the ground.

An arrow flew over Marcellus' head. He now spied two archers in the camp, one with an empty bow and one grabbing an arrow from a pack. The other bandit from the camp was now mounted and charging toward Marcellus, sword in hand. Marcellus quickly turned around, switched his shield to his left arm, drew his sword, and charged at the bandit who had been thrown from his horse. Dazed, the man barely looked up before Marcellus' sword swept across his neck. The other bandit on the road sped away. An arrow flew over Marcellus, and another planted itself in his shield.

Marcellus spun around, but only had time to raise his shield and block the sword coming down on him. The blow was hard enough to nearly knock him off his horse. As if on cue, Kopto reared and struck the bandit's horse on its flank. The injured horse jerked up violently. Marcellus slashed at the bandit's back as he fell off. The ground turned red around the lifeless body.

An arrow grazed Marcellus' exposed shoulder while another flew over his head. His spear was within reach, sticking out of the bandit's chest. Marcellus yanked it out and quickly charged down the shallow grade toward one of the archers. The man panicked and ran. Marcellus and his horse were upon him quickly, and the spear went through another chest.

When Marcellus turned around, he saw the last bandit on his knees, yelling and weeping. "Have mercy on me! Have mercy on me!" Marcellus rode slowly toward the man, making sure that there was no trap. As he got closer, the man buried his forehead in the dirt and continued to shout, "Have mercy on me! Have mercy on me!"

Marcellus dismounted and grabbed his sword. In the middle of a "Have mercy on me!", Marcellus kicked the man in the back of his head and silently tied up his arms and legs.

* * *

At first, Marcellus was not surprised by anything he found in the camp. There were several coins, small household items made of silver and gold, some weapons, food, wine, water, and feed for the horses. There were several wineskins and pouches full of plants and powders that Marcellus could not identify.

He did not expect to find dragons, however. He first saw them crudely etched into pieces of leather and wood. Another was inked onto the lone piece of parchment that he found. As he stacked the bodies of the four men he had killed and fought off the combined odors of smoke and unwashed skin, he noticed that each had a faded but recognizable dragon tattooed on the left arm. The tattoos were all the same, showing a greenish creature with a long tail that curled into its open mouth. Its head was large and snakelike; its blank eyes were red. While searching the unconscious bandit for weapons, he saw a dragon tattoo on the bandit's left arm and another on his back.

By the time the bandit began to wake, Marcellus had rounded up the horses. He killed two: one was diseased and the other had been badly injured by Kopto. He generously fed and watered the other horses. The bandit looked with surprise as Marcellus stoked the fire and silently prepared two plates of food and poured two goblets of wine.

Marcellus broke the silence. "Are you hungry?"

The bandit nodded.

"Do not move." Marcellus cut through the rope binding the man's hands. He handed the bandit a goblet. "Drink something first." The man obeyed as Marcellus ate some food. "If you want something to eat," said Marcellus while holding up the other plate, "answer my questions. First, how long have you been thieving?"

"Many years," the man answered.

"Are there no soldiers nearby? How do you get away with it? You six weren't much of a match for even one soldier."

"Cephalus is the local army officer. We give him gold and silver and he lets us control the road." He stopped to finish his wine. "We also give him information about the travelers we encounter."

Marcellus' heart sank. He thought of all the soldiers under his command and what they wished for: a home, some money, peace, and a Rome that was great. They did not fight to help bandits like these.

The bandit's head wobbled slightly as he continued talking. "Cephalus is a dragon-worshipper, too. He would not give us so much freedom if he did not worship the dragon."

Marcellus eyed the bandit. The wine is having an effect, he thought. I had better get information from him now before it alters him even more.

"What nonsense!" he said roughly. "Dragons and dragon-worship. You and this Cephalus want gold, that's all."

The man stared at Marcellus with bright, wild eyes. His voice quivered. "You do not understand! The dragon is so wise, so strong. He is beautiful! I was a slave when he told me to join these bandits."

"Then you are still a slave," Marcellus gruffed.

"No, the dragon set me free! Cephalus knows this, too. I bowed to the dragon once. Cephalus talks with him all the time. If you only knew about...what..."

The bandit blinked slowly several times, then fell forward. Marcellus sighed. The thought of killing the bandit crossed his mind, but he simply threw the plate of food into a nearby clump of bushes and let the bandit lie there. A mouthful of dirt and an empty stomach will be enough trouble for him, he thought.

Marcellus loaded the small treasures in a few packs and tied them onto the newly captured horses. He roped the horses together and attached the rope to Kopto's saddle. A nice gift for my father, he thought with satisfaction.

As he wondered whether the rest of his journey would be safe, he made a vow. "Immortal gods," he said in a low voice, "I will drive officers like Cephalus out of the army when I am promoted. I will make the great Roman Empire even greater."

He mounted Kopto and led the other horses toward his father's estate.

CHAPTER THREE

A MEAL WITH HIS FATHER

"The food is excellent, father. And the wine..." Marcellus' voice trailed off as he contentedly drained a goblet.

Titus smiled and tipped his own goblet. "Perhaps you are simply dulled by military food."

"No, father. This would be excellent anywhere, anytime."

Marcellus was enjoying his fourth day at his father's estate. By slow degrees, the familiar sounds and scenery of the estate had been like an invisible hand lifting heavy burdens from his shoulders. Here, he had no soldiers to watch or order, no superiors to report to. He did not even have to care for Kopto, though he made sure to visit and ride him every day. And although he had not thought much about his wedding, he knew that planning it would be relaxing compared to managing military affairs.

He had noticed some changes at the estate. The place was busier, bigger, and obviously more successful than ever. There were more crops, more animals, bigger orchards, more slaves, and more workers.

One change surprised and puzzled him, however. When he rode past a dry ravine on the edge of the estate after his second day back,

---

he saw no bodies there. His family had always called this place the "slave ditch," for that is where they threw the bodies of slaves that had died. When he was growing up, only a handful of slaves lived on the estate, but it was still rare when none had died within the past year. Now, it seemed as if there were slaves everywhere. Some even had families. He recognized some as defeated soldiers from his raids, but most of the new ones seemed to have been acquired by his father. Still, the ditch was empty.

His father had also changed in three years. The ring of hair on his head was grayer and thinner, and the wrinkles on his face were deeper and longer. His head stooped forward unnaturally. But his eyes have life, thought Marcellus. They shone with measured pride as he talked about the success of the estate. They focused squarely on whomever he was talking to. And at this moment, they delighted in the food, wine, and conversation of a midday meal with his only child.

Most of the activity on the estate was unchanged, however. His father still read every morning – "usually Cicero," he said. Then, he discussed the estate's affairs with Pasikrates, the slave who had managed it since before Marcellus was born. And Pasikrates, although grayer around his temples, was still cheerful, energetic, and devoted to Marcellus' father. The large fountain in the courtyard still gurgled gently, the bathhouse still provided hot, luxurious relaxation, and his bed was much more comfortable than anything he slept on as an army officer.

His father lay back on some pillows with his goblet in hand. "You have not said much about army life, my son. What is happening on the eastern frontier? What is the Emperor Diocletian planning – or, I should say, the Emperor Diocletian and the Caesar Galerius, now that Diocletian wants to divide the empire."

"You are not in favor of the plan, father?"

"By the gods, no! Please do not say you are."

"No, father, although I have not given it much thought. Emperors and Caesars are military men of high rank, and military men of high rank are always looking to achieve a higher rank. The Caesars will want to be emperors, and the emperors will want to dominate each other. It is a recipe for war, I think."

Marcellus' father raised his eyebrows slightly and smiled. "Precisely. Now, tell me about the eastern border. Are you still worried about the Sassanids? Or is it the Armenians now? Have you been unsuccessful recently? Except what you brought me a few days ago, I have only received one slave and a handful of treasure in the past year."

Marcellus smiled too. "You forget father, that men of rank, to stay men of rank, need to be generous to their own men first, especially their officers. You will love me no matter what I send you or do not send you. My men need their rewards before they respect me."

The old man's eyes relaxed as he laughed quietly and nodded. "Of course. And as you see, I am not in need of anything."

"Right now," Marcellus continued, "we are holding both the Sassanids and the Armenians where they belong."

"How many killed in your last raid?"

"Dozens, perhaps a hundred."

"And you personally?"

"Twelve at least, but – "

"But it was dark," interrupted Marcellus' father. "Remember, my son, who made sure you learned to be a soldier."

As the old man leaned over to refill his son's goblet, Marcellus silently acknowledged that his father had taught him most of what he knew about being a soldier. It had started with stories. He remembered listening to his father recount the deeds of the legendary warriors: Achilles, Odysseus, Hector, and especially Aeneas, the founder of Rome. He also remembered the stories of his father's own raids and campaigns, and now that he was an experienced soldier himself, he realized that even the grand stories were probably true. In fact, Marcellus still longed to match his father's capture of a Persian general – along with 50 soldiers and slaves – and parade them before a long line of Roman soldiers and citizens.

His favorite stories had been the ones about the great Roman army: Julius Caesar's campaigns against the Gauls and his daring crossing of the Rubicon River, the slow but steady triumph over Carthage, Hadrian's conquest and great wall in Britannia, Scipio's defeat of Hannibal in Africa. "All the things we enjoy now," his father would always say at the end of such stories, "we owe to the Roman army." He didn't have to add, "and that's why I'm an officer in Rome's great army."

The stories had inspired Marcellus as he excelled in his early training. His father taught him only a few things because he was so often away with the army, but he had arranged for a series of men to instruct him. Caspius and Maximus for boxing, Brontius for archery, Leontitus for horsemanship. When Marcellus was ten years old, a recently acquired slave –a former officer in the Persian army, Pasikrates had said – taught him both Persian and Roman battle tactics.

When Marcellus was sixteen years old, he began his army training. His superiors quickly noticed his skills and extensive knowledge of military strategy and concluded that their training would be wasted on him. He was immediately sent on minor raids and reconnaissance missions against the Sassanids. On these missions, he learned about the raw emotions of war and how to govern himself and others in intense situations. Within two years, he was leading these missions. Within five years, he was named a tribune and given over one hundred men to command.

"Yes, father," said Marcellus after finishing his wine. "I remember who made me a soldier. And I am grateful." He looked directly into his father's eyes and felt an unspoken love and admiration pass between them. "I only hope Galerius does not ruin the army while I am in it," he said in an attempt to lighten the moment.

His father laughed. "A fool with a fool's errand. I have heard he is trying to eradicate Christians from the empire, starting with the army."

"Not yet, father, but Demetrios has warned me that it is coming. Many of my best soldiers and officers are Christians."

His father angrily rose from his pillows and began pacing. His eyes were darkened by his furrowed brows. "And three of every four slaves on this estate are as well, including Pasikrates. Does Galerius not realize that Christians are everywhere in the empire? Does he not see that they are generally good, peaceful, honest men and women?" He stopped and stared at Marcellus. "Do you know that Pasikrates even turned down freedom in the name of this Christ?"

Marcellus frowned. "You offered Pasikrates his freedom?"

His father shrugged. "He has served our household for many years. But he said no! He even wept when he said that he did not want to break fellowship with his brother slaves. I was too surprised to ask him anything at the time. I offered him his freedom again, and he said the same thing. He is a good man who wants to remain a slave – so let him be a slave, I thought. But Galerius!" He paced again. "Pasikrates is the kind of man he wants to destroy. Fool!"

"But father, these Christians reject Roman custom when they do not worship the gods. I remember Cicero writing that the gods love nothing more than people living by law and custom together. He would not tolerate Christians living on his estate, would he?"

"Cicero did not live in these times. He would be prudent, like I am. People say that I allow slaves to be Christians because your mother was Christian, but I do it for order and stability on the estate. Custom is important, but I say as long as people respect the laws and the emperor, let them be Christians, children of Hermes, Jews, Zoroastrians, or even dragon worshippers."

Marcellus looked up in surprise, but a slave entered the room before he could say anything. "A gift from Regina, for the master Marcellus," the slave declared.

Marcellus rose, took the small, circular object wrapped in some kind of skin, and waved the slave out of the room. A small string encircled the wrapping twice and was tied off in a bow. Marcellus turned the gift over, feeling a heavy, circular object through the smooth exterior. He unwrapped it and found himself staring into the jeweled eyes of a dragon.

For what seemed like a long time, Marcellus felt transfixed by those eyes. They were dark red and shimmered as if they were sunlight dyed in blood. The dragon itself was silver. Its scales sloped intricately along a body that gradually thinned as it wrapped upon itself. The forked tail nearly touched the forked tongue inside the dragon's slightly open mouth. The dragon's face was laced with smaller, more intricate scales, bearing an expression that was fierce and determined. Combined with the fire-blood eyes, the dragon seemed ready to bellow smoke from its nostrils.

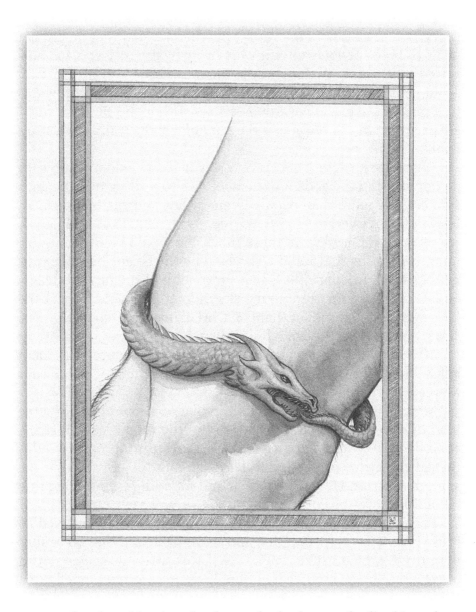

"Its scales sloped intricately along a body that gradually thinned as it wrapped upon itself."

"Exquisite," murmured Titus. Marcellus jumped. He had not noticed his father moving closer to him.

"Exquisite and beautiful," replied Marcellus softly. He traced the dragon's circular body with his fingers and felt the cold weight of the silver press against his hand. Strength and suppleness, he thought. He gazed again at the eyes. He felt that if he gave himself to those eyes, he would be slowly eaten and fulfilled at the same time. And yet they are so beautiful, he thought. "And terrible," he said aloud to his father.

His father half-snorted and half-chuckled. "Terrible, but only if you believe in that sort of thing, as your future wife obviously does. I recommend that you wear that tomorrow when you see her."

His father's tone broke Marcellus' gaze into the dragon's eyes. He noticed that the silver dragon was, in fact, an armband with a smooth underbelly on the bottom and realistically rough scales on top. He slipped it on easily. It was heavy but comfortable, and it stayed in place halfway between his elbow and his shoulder.

"Yes, I will," said Marcellus, "it will please her." He paused. "What does this represent, though? Demetrios mentioned some rumors about a dragon in this region, and you mention something about dragon worshippers."

Titus laughed loudly. "It is the ignorance of slaves, the silliness of the rich, and the superstitions of both. But if it is no harm to the empire, leave it alone, I say." He paused briefly, then eyed Marcellus with a grin. "Even if you are marrying into it."

"But father, if there is no real dragon, what do these people, these dragon worshippers, actually do? Who are they?"

"Slaves mostly, along with some rich women like your future wife. Maybe others. It does not seem to be an organized type of worship. I have heard that people go to a cave beyond Lucius' estate and make sacrifices. I have also heard of some writings, but I have not seen anything. A few of my slaves – our slaves, I should say – asked me for a goat to sacrifice, saying that they would mention my name to the dragon. I told them that I only sacrificed to the gods and the emperor and my ancestors. They grumbled, but they have not asked again. They are the type of slaves you have to keep an eye on – lazy and petty thieves. And they do not get along with the Christians."

Marcellus remembered the dragons among the bandits, especially the red eyes on the tattoos. He decided against mentioning the bandits to his father. Not now, he thought. We can discuss it after the wedding. But he was more curious than ever about this practice.

"So you will leave tomorrow for Lucius' estate to see your future wife?" asked Titus.

Marcellus nodded. "I will talk with her about this dragon worship. And the wedding, of course. And other things, surely. I will send a message if I choose to stay overnight. I am sure Lucius will invite me."

He removed the armband and gazed at it. He marveled again at the combination of strength and suppleness suggested by the body and the transfixing eyes. He wanted to know more about this metal dragon. He shuddered slightly at the thought of meeting a real dragon. What would it say? What could it do?

"Father," he began, but felt an unnatural silence around him. When he finally looked up, his father had gone. He looked again at the armband. The red eyes, he again felt, were trying to devour and fulfill him.

CHAPTER FOUR

A FEAST IN HIS HONOR

As he rode past the slave ditch on his way to Lucius' estate, Marcellus reprimanded himself. He had meant to ask his father why the slave ditch was empty, but talk of Galerius, Christians, and the dragon had distracted him.

I have at least thirty days left, thought Marcellus. I'll find out soon enough.

Lucius' estate soon came into view. Like Titus' estate, it had a substantial array of crops, a large herd of cows along with some other livestock, and slaves working everywhere. Lucius had inherited a small farm with a half-dozen slaves and, while successfully trading jewels for twenty years, expanded it to a fair-sized estate with more than one hundred slaves. Although not as large as Titus' estate, it was big enough to lift Lucius into the higher tiers of Roman society and to attract merchants from places such as Egypt and Sicily. Marcellus suspected that one of those merchants had crafted the dragon resting on his forearm.

Marcellus always felt uncomfortable on Lucius' estate, but did not know why. As he rode toward the estate house, he admired the crops and the busy slaves in the fields. He saw that a new building was going up at the edge of the fields. New living quarters for slaves, no doubt, thought Marcellus. Sturdy and efficient, just like Lucius. And what was wrong with sturdiness and efficiency? He always wanted to see more of such things in his own soldiers.

But right past the new slave dwelling, along the road, was another sign of Lucius' efficiency. A young man's body hung from a post. Flies swarmed around it, and an awful odor extended to Marcellus' nose. The man's back had been ravaged, probably by a whip. Marcellus rode past quickly.

Perhaps that is it, Marcellus thought. Lucius is harsh with his slaves. Titus used discipline when necessary, but his estate was not known for the regular beatings, whippings, and executions that came to characterize Lucius' estate as he grew richer.

And it is no mistake, Marcellus continued to think, that the dead young man was placed where slaves away from Lucius' gaze would notice. "I will be glad to be the master of my father's estate and not this one," he said to himself.

* * *

A surprising commotion erupted when Marcellus arrived at the villa. Slaves began scurrying in all directions. Many people appeared and looked at him with curiosity. Some of these people were clearly not Roman, although all appeared remarkably clean and well-fed. Instead of traditional light-colored Roman togas and dresses, they wore clothes in a panorama of colors – turbans, robes, and military-looking outfits. Many wore elaborate makeup, even some of the men. All wore glittering jewelry.

"Marcellus!" called Lucius' high voice. He and at least a dozen slaves swept in from one of the many hallways. Two of the slaves fanned with branches and two carried scrolls of some sort; the rest had no obvious purpose.

Lucius ran up and embraced Marcellus, then grabbed Marcellus' arm and turned to his guests. "My good friends!" announced Lucius.

"This is Marcellus, my neighbor, my fellow citizen, my friend, and my future son-in-law!"

All around the villa, people clapped and cheered. Marcellus reddened slightly, but made a polite bow. He knew that Lucius wanted everyone to see him, so he stood squarely and held his head high.

"Now that he is here," Lucius continued, "I can confidently say that we will have a great wedding feast in –" He paused and whispered to Marcellus, "Ten days?" Marcellus smiled and nodded, and Lucius completed his sentence for everyone else: "Ten days!" The guests clapped and cheered again. Lucius had to hold up his hand to quiet them.

"This man is, as you probably know, a tribune in our great Roman army, and I hear –" he half-turned to Marcellus "– that he will certainly rise higher than tribune. Galerius himself has his eyes on this man, even though he is obviously not very good at obeying the rules about soldiers getting married!"

Laughter erupted as Lucius beamed. He waited before holding up his hands again. "Now I know how much business needs to be done, my friends, but I have been waiting for a long time for Marcellus to come. Today, no more business. Instead, we will feast in honor of Marcellus!"

The guests erupted in cheers again, and then everyone moved rapidly. Ten of the slaves surrounding Lucius scurried down the hallway from which they had entered. Some of the guests hastened toward the family's part of the building – presumably, Marcellus thought with some amusement, because they think they need to change clothes and find new jewelry to wear. The rest of the guests bustled in the direction of Lucius' dining hall, chattering and sometimes bumping into one another in their rush to get to the feast.

Lucius turned to Marcellus. "You will sit next to me. Everyone here can be helpful in your career, so I want you to meet all of them."

The feast revealed to Marcellus another reason why he was never at ease on Lucius' estate. The food and wine were excellent, and Lucius had arranged for musicians and dancers throughout the meal. The guests were loud, however, and only got louder and more disorderly as the feast went on. After meeting with several merchants of jewels, dyed cloth, and other fineries, he and Lucius and the guests reclined on the couches and began the meal. The guests and even Lucius himself ate and drank so voraciously and rapidly that the slaves were running in and out of the room with platters of food and jugs of wine. Marcellus thought about his father, quietly reading Cicero every morning, managing his estate calmly, and upbraiding family members for not learning self-control. He looked at the increasingly drunken guests. No one here reads Cicero, he thought.

As more empty jugs lined the walls, the guests got louder and less careful with their words.

"Merchants are the backbone of the empire, not soldiers," growled one voice. "Let's see a soldier try to fill the emperor's treasury."

"If he can get married, what other orders can he disobey?" asked another voice.

"Christians! I say more power to Galerius. The fewer of them the better!" shouted another.

"We'll have to find Lucius' wine cellar one of these nights," another stated in a failed whisper.

Not wanting to insult Lucius, Marcellus did his best to pretend that he heard none of these comments. He also ignored the outbursts among a few of the guests, one of which resulted in blows. Lucius was able to convince these guests to separate and take more wine and food.

One remark in particular caught Marcellus' attention. He heard a half-drunken voice say, "If the dragon says so, it is probably right." He looked to see where it had come from, but heard nothing else. He also noticed that most of the guests and slaves gazed at his armband but said nothing. Only Lucius acknowledged it, saying, "We had that made especially for you."

It was Lucius' daughter Regina who made the feast interesting for Marcellus. She said only formal words to him when she entered the room: "Greetings, Marcellus, and welcome." But her beauty and command of the situation constantly attracted his attention. She attended to her many guests, was surrounded by a half-dozen slaves at all times, and was almost always in conversation. She ate and drank sparingly. As the feast went on and the guests became

"It was Lucius' daughter Regina who made the feast interesting for Marcellus."

more raucous, she remained calm, attentive, and polite. She moved about the room gracefully and captured Marcellus' gaze with her dark eyes more than once. There was even a hint of longing in the look, Marcellus thought. Not desperate longing, but intense, as if she were trying to ask an important question across the room.

Once, as Regina talked to a guest near Marcellus, he caught the glint of something on her arm. When he looked more closely, he saw a maze of subtle, overlapping scales and deep, ruby eyes. She had an armband exactly like his. Then he found that she was looking at him. She glanced at her armband and at his armband before smiling as if she had an important secret to share. But then a guest called her name, and she moved to the other side of the room.

He did not speak to her until the sun began setting. She strode confidently to her father and said, somewhat loudly, "Father, I think Marcellus should be our guest tonight as well."

Smiling, Lucius looked about until he met her gaze with his bloodshot eyes. It took him a few moments to comprehend the words. But he soon raised his eyes to Marcellus. "Yes, of course, stay as long as you like."

Marcellus rose quickly. "Lucius and Regina, my thanks for your hospitality, but my father..."

"... is probably being informed as we speak," said Regina with a smile. "I sent word to him a while ago. Surely your good father can manage the estate in your absence."

Marcellus bowed and could not help but smile back at her. "It seems as if I am a prisoner of your hospitality."

"But of course. I trust that you will be a happy prisoner."

"Yes, very happy. My gratitude, Regina."

Regina leaned down to kiss her father, then leaned toward Marcellus. "I will see you tonight," she whispered.

Marcellus was surprised. No other party had been planned, and Lucius certainly would not be talking with him until the next day. What business had to be discussed that night, and why would Regina be the one discussing it?

Regina stood up and walked away before he could say anything. He looked up and, before she left the room, caught the glint of the evening sun's rays reflecting off the dragon on her arm.

CHAPTER FIVE

A MEETING WITH REGINA

Regina came to Marcellus long after all the other guests had gone to bed.

Marcellus was reading a book with the help of two candles. Lucius started collecting books when he became richer. As far as Marcellus could tell, however, he had touched none. The copy of Cicero's treatise on friendship was the finest Marcellus had seen. He was struggling to understand the words of a Platonist philosopher about beauty when he heard a rapping on his doorway.

Marcellus looked up, surprised. Maybe it is a slave with some more wine, he thought. "Marcellus here."

"And Regina here," came a smooth voice.

As she entered, Marcellus hurriedly stood up and wrapped his cloak around his shoulders to look more formal. Regina was wearing a white dress with a glittering fabric laced onto the neck, back, and waist. With the exception of a lock dangling by each ear, her hair was firmly tied up in an elaborate series of interlocking strands and curls. Two rings on each hand reflected the candlelight. As she walked toward Marcellus, he caught the glint of the ruby dragon eyes from her armband.

"You are alone, Regina? No slaves?"

"One, behind me in the hall, my husband and lord," she said while looking at him with smiling eyes. She knelt down in front of him, and he was forced to inhale a thin cloud of perfume. He took a step back.

"You do not like those titles, Marcellus?" she asked with a smile.

"No – I mean yes, yes," Marcellus sputtered, "but it is just, it is just not the time. I mean, we should not be alone together, Regina, even with a slave in the hallway. Please stand up."

Regina laughed a silvery, rounded laugh as she rose. She did not hesitate to lock her eyes into Marcellus'. He saw again the longing he had seen at the feast, an eagerness that was more than simple desire or anxiousness. She closed her eyes and, before he could move back, leaned forward and kissed him softly on the cheek.

Marcellus closed his own eyes and breathed in deeply. He wished for another kiss, but managed to say, "This is your father's house."

Another silvery laugh. When Marcellus opened his eyes, he saw Regina reclining on some pillows.

"I will not stay long. Do not be afraid, Marcellus. What am I saying! As if you, a noble soldier of Rome, could be afraid of me. I only want you to do something for me."

The only place to recline was on the pillows next to Regina. Marcellus hesitated slightly, but he did not want to displease his future wife. And there was, after all, a slave in the hallway.

Regina again looked into Marcellus' eyes. "Did you enjoy the feast today?"

"It was an honor."

Another light, rounded laugh. "You are most graciously dishonest. All of the other guests drank endless goblets of wine, and you were probably thinking about coming here to read that book."

She held out her hand to him and he took it. It occurred to him that he could not remember a time that he had not known her. They were born less than a year apart and both became motherless at a young age, so their slave-caretakers had an easy time convincing their fathers to let them play with each other regularly.

And even then, he recalled, she liked to playfully ignore rules. He remembered a picnic with Regina and their two slave attendants. While the slaves were busy nattering among themselves, Regina had leaned over to Marcellus and whispered "follow me." As Marcellus got up, she walked nonchalantly toward a thicket. When one of the slaves yelled, "Regina and Marcellus, come back now!", she grabbed Marcellus' arm and pulled him into a thin gap between two bushes.

"Over there!" she said as Marcellus fought off branches and tried to ignore the growing number of scratches on his legs and arms. He saw a large rock through the thinning thicket. Regina let go of his arm and sprinted to the other side of it. He followed and found her crouching down with her back against the rock. Regina looked at him and held her finger to her mouth but giggled through it.

"Marcellus! Regina!" came the voices of the slaves, followed by grunts, curses, and brush being pushed aside. Regina giggled harder. "Regina and Marcellus, come here now!"

Regina suddenly stopped giggling. She looked at Marcellus, then peered into a darker, thicker part of the forest that lay ahead of them. Still looking ahead, she slowly reached over and grabbed his hand. Then her grip tightened. Before he could say anything, she lunged toward the darkness. Not wanting to pull his hand away, he jumped forward and nearly knocked over the slave who had just stepped from around the rock. The other slave appeared and grabbed Regina. She resisted briefly, but then descended into more giggles. She looked at Marcellus again, obviously happy despite her torn clothes and the scratches on her arms and legs. Marcellus couldn't help smiling back, and he smiled again as he recalled this memory.

As they grew older, they saw one another often. Before either came of age, their fathers were talking of marriage, especially as Lucius became wealthier and began living as a high-born Roman citizen. Even before Marcellus left for the army, the size of Regina's dowry had been determined, and all that remained was for Marcellus to reach the rank of tribune. When that occurred, word was sent for Marcellus to take his leave at his convenience.

I am glad I like her, thought Marcellus. And she will certainly be able to manage the estate while I am gone. Even father will be glad of her help and company.

"Yes, I thought of these books," said Marcellus, "but I also enjoyed the wonderful food and wine. It was obviously a very important event for your father. And I met people from all over the Empire, even some Egyptians and Sassanids."

Another silvery laugh. "Father's mastery of jewels makes him many friends indeed. He always seems to be making more friends. Were any of them interested in the army?"

"Everyone was polite," Marcellus answered carefully, "but..."

"They were more interested in the wonderful food and wine?" finished Regina as she eyed him playfully.

"Precisely," Marcellus smiled. He decided to surprise her. "Watching you, in fact, was the only true enjoyment of the feast."

Regina raised her eyebrows and blushed slightly before looking away briefly. When she looked back at Marcellus, she had her playful smile again. To his surprise, she let go of his hand and stroked the scales on his armband from head to tail. "I see you got your present."

"It is exquisite, Regina, and I am delighted that you have one as well."

Again to his surprise, Regina gripped his hand and looked at him with a new, fierce longing. Leaning in close, she whispered intensely, "That is why I came to see you tonight, Marcellus. To tell you about the dragon."

Marcellus wanted to reply, but thought that it was best to let her talk. She continued to hold his hand tightly, and he remembered a similar grip from when she was about to plunge deeper into the forest.

"I heard of the dragon a year ago," she began, "although the dragon says he has been there much longer. Some new jewel traders arrived. One was Egyptian and the other an exiled Parthian. They were different from the other traders. They kept to themselves and sometimes could not be found in the middle of the day. The slaves whispered that they performed rituals at night and even stole animals for sacrifices. They did not always attend father's feasts, and when they did, they ate only a little and never got drunk.

"I was curious, and of course I wanted to know if my father and I could trust these men. So I sent a slave to follow them. When he came back that evening, he was trembling. He was a clumsy slave, so the traders had caught him not too far from the estate. He was also somewhat stupid, so he told them everything, of course. The traders talked among themselves and agreed to bring him to the dragon. The dragon was not too far away, just over the hill and beyond to the cave at the bottom of the cliff – I am sure you know the place.

"He breathlessly told of the trip. The two traders stripped his horse, which was shaking terribly and could barely be restrained. The traders started chanting something odd and dark in a language my slave could not recognize. Smoke came out of the cave, then a head, then a long, sinewy body. It was a dragon! My slave could not move, and the horse was also petrified with fear. As the two traders kept chanting, the dragon crept to the horse, knocked it down, then started devouring it. The slave fainted. He told me that he thought he was going to be eaten too.

"When the slave woke up, he was here. The traders had draped him over one of their horses. They had him tell me that I could go with them the next day. He came to me immediately, told me everything, and then – I did not understand this at the time – begged to go with me. He even promised to pay for an animal to sacrifice."

Regina's eager eyes rested on Marcellus. From many hours of negotiations with enemy commanders, he had learned to listen without betraying any emotions, so he stared at her impassively even though he was intensely interested. A flicker crossed her face. Was that anger? wondered Marcellus. But she quickly smiled.

"I am not boring you, am I?"

"No, of course not. Did you see it? Was there really a dragon there?"

She leaned toward Marcellus, her eyes full of excitement. She squeezed his hand even harder. "There was, oh my dear Marcellus, there was! He talked to me, he asked me to bring another sacrifice." She closed her eyes. "He breathed on me."

Marcellus felt her hand tremble. Her eyes were still closed. "I have talked with him more, many, many times. His wisdom is...it is..." She couldn't finish her sentence. Slowly, her eyes opened up, unlocking a fierce gaze at Marcellus. "I have told him everything. He approves of our marriage. He wants to meet you."

Marcellus was surprised. "Why?"

"Because I want you to meet him."

Her eyes were still full of eagerness and longing. Like a young soldier eager for battle, thought Marcellus, and with the same need for assurance.

Marcellus put his other hand on top of Regina's and said, "As I wish to please you, I will meet this dragon."

Regina brought her cheek next to Marcellus'. Her perfume enveloped his sense of smell. He could feel wetness on her cheeks. Her breathing did not sound tense, but relieved.

"My dear Marcellus," she whispered. She started to say more, but gave herself over to tears instead.

CHAPTER SIX

THE DRAGON

Marcellus did not sleep well and, as he rode away from Lucius' estate, he could not banish uneasiness from his mind. What was a dragon – or whatever it was – doing in this region? Was it a threat to his father's estate? Were there other fantastic creatures throughout the empire? And what about the bandits and the army commander who were supposedly in the creature's service?

He had his hunting knife with him, but he knew that such a weapon, even if well-made, could not help him against a creature that could eat a horse or a man. Still, he felt sure that he was in no danger. If the creature had not harmed the traders, Regina, Regina's slave, or even the bandits, it would not harm him.

But the uneasiness remained and even grew as the landscape changed. Plush, grassy fields slowly gave way to weedy, rocky terrain. The well-beaten path curved more often as it went over small ridges and around the occasional dead tree, like a snake winding its way through blackened underbrush. Kopto was also uneasy. He shook his mane and whinnied for no reason, and Marcellus had to spur him to keep a steady pace.

Marcellus stopped when he saw a strange, whitish-gray rock on the side of the path. As he clambered off Kopto, he took in a quick breath when he realized that it was a large bone, probably from a horse or a cow. He noticed several ragged ridges embedded in the bone. Teeth marks, he realized. As he turned to lead Kopto on foot, he noticed many more bones scattered randomly along the sides of the path. It was as if an animal graveyard had suddenly convulsed its contents to the surface.

Marcellus took a deep breath and patted Kopto's neck. "It is just over that ridge ahead," he spoke softly, "so steady, boy, steady."

Marcellus' eye wandered over the landscape as he and Kopto moved along the path. Green plants had disappeared almost entirely, replaced by blackheaded reeds and dirt. In some places, it seemed as if fire had spread. And bones were everywhere. Some had the tell-tale grooves, others were surrounded by black birds fighting each other. Marcellus recognized an entire rib cage, again from a cow or a horse, but most of the other bones were scattered and broken beyond recognition.

As Marcellus came to the top of a cliff, he saw the path that snaked down a large, steep hill to a desolate plain. Further along the bottom of the cliff, he spotted a dark opening. He could see hundreds of bones and birds near it. He patted Kopto's neck again and made his way down the path.

* * *

When he got to the plain, the stench of rotting flesh accompanied the ashen landscape. The smell was surrounded by stillness. The birds were nearly silent, and no other living creatures could be seen or heard. The only sounds came from the soft crunch of Marcellus' feet and Kopto's hooves. Marcellus felt as if the breeze had stopped blowing long before he got there.

Kopto resisted Marcellus' lead as they moved closer to the cave. Once, the horse threw his head up as if trying to escape.

"Easy, Kopto," said Marcellus gently.

But Marcellus had trouble feeling calm himself. The bread and cheese he had eaten in the morning churned in his stomach. As he saw and smelled the bones and the birds, he remembered the dead bodies piled in the sun after his first battle.

Kopto reared up again when Marcellus tried to move closer to the cave. Marcellus staggered back to control him. When he tried to lead Kopto forward again, Kopto simply would not advance. Every time Marcellus pulled on the reins, Kopto whinnied as if imploring Marcellus to turn back. Marcellus knew that Kopto was not a horse that shied away from battle. He also knew that this was different.

He patted Kopto again on the neck. "Stay here, boy. I will go alone from here."

Although no breeze blew, piles of ashes, some still hot, showered the air with dust and stench. No birds were interested in the carcasses nearest to the cave. Marcellus moved uneasily forward until he was close to the cave entrance. He could feel heat coming out of it on his face and limbs. He also smelled something new: not the stench of smoldering flesh, but of an unwashed animal and piles of dung.

Marcellus reeled slightly from the barren and foul assault upon his senses. The general dread in his heart grew. But his training and experience allowed him to keep his wits about him, even though he did not know what to do. He stood there, waiting, feeling his heart beat. Then a low voice came from the cave. "Hello, Marcellus," it said.

Although facing the cave, Marcellus whirled about and drew his knife. Recognizing his folly, he turned back to face the cave. He heard a low, smooth chuckle with a hint of a hiss. "Really, Marcellus," came the voice again, "do you think you could harm a dragon with that? Do not be afraid. I will not harm you."

Marcellus did not put the knife away. Slowly, a leathery, scaled, dark gray claw with three yellowed talons came out of the cave. Each talon was large, about the size of Marcellus' foot. Then another claw emerged. Then a head.

Marcellus drew in a quick breath. The dragon's eyes were like those of his armband: red and lustrous and bottomless. Marcellus wanted to look away, but he could not. He backed away a few steps.

"Marcellus, do not be afraid," said the dragon. "I only want to talk with you."

The dragon blinked, and Marcellus was able to look elsewhere. The dragon's sinewy, scaly body came out of the cave, haphazardly absorbing and reflecting the hazy sunlight. It was green, but not like the green on the bandits' tattoos. Many greens undulated in and out of existence as the scales moved, again transfixing Marcellus' eyes. "Wings," thought Marcellus as he gazed at the dark interruptions along the dragon's side. The dragon continued to emerge, revealing two more claws with six more talons and a tail nearly as long as the body.

The dragon moved closer to Marcellus, who could not decide if it was walking or slithering. He was fascinated by its steady, curving advance. He caught the dragon's eyes and again could not look away.

"You are quite rude, Marcellus," said the dragon. The voice was still low and smooth. "I have said hello to you and you have said nothing. You will not even put your knife away." The dragon breathed in and out loudly, as if sighing. It was so close to Marcellus that he felt its hot breath on his face. The smoky, foul odor of the dragon's breath combined with the other smells to make Marcellus cough and almost wretch. The dragon noticed.

"The smell, is it, Marcellus? That is why Kopto would not come any closer. Do not worry. You will get used to it. Everybody does. Some even come to love it."

Marcellus flinched. Had Regina told this dragon his horse's name? What else did this creature know? He was about to ask, but the dragon spoke first.

"Still nothing to say, Marcellus? You have not retreated, so you must want to be here, unlike your horse." This comment was followed by a snort and a low rumble that sounded like a bellied chuckle. "Well, I suppose you need to feel safe in order to talk."

Before Marcellus could say anything or even move, the dragon dove forward and wrapped its tail around him. It did not grip or even touch him, but the scales hovered near Marcellus on all sides.

"Before Marcellus could say anything or even move, the dragon dove forward and wrapped its tail around him."

The dragon raised its head and looked directly at Marcellus. Again, Marcellus' stomach turned and he stifled an urge to choke. "Now," the creature said, "try to hurt me with your knife."

Marcellus did not move.

"Look at me, Marcellus." Something in Marcellus hinted that he shouldn't, but he obeyed. "Now hurt me with your knife."

Marcellus felt that he could not refuse. The dragon bent its head down, and Marcellus raised his knife with both hands and drove it downward. Instead of piercing the neck, the knife grazed off the scales, and Marcellus nearly lost his balance.

This time, the dragon's laughter was unmistakable. "Try again."

Marcellus tried again, with the same result. The dragon's body again rippled with laughter. With the laughter came small plumes of smoke and large amounts of hot, decrepit air. Marcellus' head spun as he breathed this in, and he again had to fight off the impulse to gag.

Think like a soldier, Marcellus told himself as he tried to take regular breaths. He scanned the dragon's body, looking for a sign of weakness. Only one point seemed vulnerable: a dark, scaleless patch of skin where the dragon's wing connected to its body. He could not reach it.

"I am waiting, Marcellus."

Wondering if he could reach the dragon's skin, Marcellus stabbed with the knife angled under a scale. The blade did not go far, but it pricked something softer than a scale, and the dragon snorted as a quiver ran throughout its body.

Marcellus noticed the reaction. "Should I try again?" he asked.

"If you wish," said the dragon in a slightly strained voice. "But it will do you no good. You see, Marcellus, I want to show that you are perfectly safe with me. You would not live one minute if I constricted you like a snake would constrict a hare. I could also chase down your beast and eat it before the sun sets. Yet I do not. Now will you put your knife away and talk with me?"

Marcellus knew that he was no match for such a beast, but the effect of the knife prick gave him some confidence. "Why did you ask to see me?" he asked in a slightly demanding tone.

The dragon stopped moving for a second, then rippled with quiet laughter. "Marcellus, you are still afraid and suspicious. I just showed you that I meant no harm."

Marcellus did not reply. The dragon broke the silence. "You are still suspicious. Let us talk on your terms, then. You are here, and you must have something you want to talk about. After all, when was the last time you got to talk with a dragon?"

As the dragon spoke, it slithered its sinewy body back and forth, sometimes even behind Marcellus. Its head, however, remained fixed on Marcellus, and it only broke contact with an occasional blink accompanied by an animal-like shake of its head and a ruffling of its wings.

Marcellus was not sure of what he should say, especially as he looked into the dragon's red eyes. Think like a soldier! he told himself.

The dragon blinked, and it suddenly occurred to Marcellus that this was like a negotiation with an enemy captain. Be strong, but show respect, he thought.

"I will talk. But I do not know how to address you. What is your name?"

A slow hiss came from the dragon's mouth, coupled with a flick of its tail. "You would not understand my name, Marcellus. Call me 'dragon.'"

Sensing an advantage, Marcellus pressed. "Why would I not understand your name?"

The dragon hissed and flicked its tail again. "I am ancient, Marcellus, more ancient than you can imagine. No one has spoken my name for thousands of years." The dragon looked away as it continued. "Not even the gods know my name, although they may think they do." The dragon looked back at Marcellus. "Call me 'dragon.'"

Marcellus was intrigued, but did not hesitate. "Very well, dragon. I wish to make an accusation, but curiosity gets the better of me. I have never seen a dragon before, so I cannot tell if you are a he-dragon or a she-dragon."

The dragon laughed so hard that smoke came out its nostrils in short bursts. "Oh Marcellus, you are so young. We dragons are not like that. We just are. When you think about it, male and female are strange and inconvenient. Is it not so?"

Marcellus hesitated and again failed to look away. The dragon spoke: "Now I will ask you a question. Why are you here?"

"Because my future wife asked me to come."

"Ah, yes, the exquisite Regina. It is always a pleasure to talk with her. She is not afraid of me."

Marcellus bristled at the indirect accusation. He decided to take the offensive. "Why did you try to kill me, dragon?" he asked forcefully.

"Kill you? Why would I kill Regina's husband?" The dragon paused, lowered its voice and locked eyes with Marcellus. "If I wanted you dead, you would be dead."

Marcellus shuddered. He tried to reply boldly, but he knew that his voice quivered. "Then what about the bandits on the road and Cephalus of the army?"

"Marcellus, you will have to explain yourself," said the dragon without pausing.

Marcellus felt a surge of anger. It is toying with me, he thought. He mastered himself, however, and carefully explained the details of his encounter with the bandits and the information he had gleaned about Cephalus. The dragon slowly bobbed its head while it listened, as if nodding.

When Marcellus was done, the dragon locked eyes with him again. "I am truly sorry, Marcellus. I thought I had made it clear to Cephalus that you were to be left alone. And he is like you: a true soldier, not one to forget an important order. I wonder..."

"Cephalus takes orders from you?" interrupted Marcellus. "What kind of soldier is he? What of his commander?"

"Words, words, Marcellus. Of course Cephalus does not take orders from me. We just talk, like you and I are talking."

"But you said—"

"Words again, Marcellus. I want to know what happened. These bandits, were they well-trained, or more like common ruffians?"

"Not well-trained at all."

"Which is why a soldier like you could kill four men, capture one, and drive away another with only a scratch to show for it. Well done, Marcellus, well done. You said there was a lot of wine in the camp?"

"Yes."

"There were strange plants and powders there as well?"

Marcellus was surprised. "How do you know this?"

The dragon chuckled again. "Marcellus, you have common soldiers under you. Are they not drawn to excess wine? And if they found some plants and spices that worked like excess wine, they would try to possess and sell them, right?"

Marcellus nodded. He did not know much about the spice trade, but he often heard stories about the intoxicating and healing powers of strange plants.

"This is my guess, Marcellus," continued the dragon. "Cephalus told these ruffians to leave you alone, but such words were lost in their drunken minds, along with simple manners to passing strangers. I will talk to Cephalus, and you will not be bothered again. He will be angry, but no matter. After all, you did the Empire a service by clearing out danger on a vital road."

Marcellus looked up. "You care about the Empire?"

"Of course, Marcellus. I was there at the beginning of the Empire. I've talked with emperors. Nero and Caligula spoke to me almost every week, and I once met Julius Caesar in the woods of Gaul. You look surprised, Marcellus."

Actually, Marcellus was shocked. "Is this true?" he asked in a hushed tone.

"I could tell you many stories. So many interesting people who have done so much for this great Empire, and most of them not emperors or generals or anyone that the historians remember. Some even gave their lives for the Empire. The Empire, Marcellus. Nothing is more important than the Empire."

Marcellus nodded, remembering Demetrios' words. Amidst his fear and his struggle to control his emotions, he felt a new kinship with the dragon. His curiosity was also stirred. "What can you tell me about these people? Did Nero really make everyone listen to his music?"

"Nero – a lost soul," the dragon sighed. "He even played for me. Most people thought that he was not a good musician, but I encouraged him. It seemed to make him happy."

"What about Mark Antony? Did he really – "

"Marcellus," interrupted the dragon, "look at the sun. We could talk about Mark Antony and Caligula and Julius Caesar until it goes down and for many days after that. But you must still ride home to your father before dark. Even now, we do not have much time. So let us talk about the things that concern us both."

Marcellus thought for a moment. "I am concerned about the Empire."

"The Empire. Yes, of course. What ails it, Marcellus?"

"Sassanids, Armenians, and German barbarians."

"Nothing else?"

"Nothing that I can think of."

The dragon slowly moved back and forth. "Yes, Marcellus. But what about the enemy within? What about those who rot the Empire from its cities and estates?"

Marcellus paused and shook his head. "Criminals, ambitious governors and bandits." He paused and thought of his conversation with his father. "Diocletian and Galerius hate Christians, but I suspect that the Christians are too unambitious to be a threat."

The dragon hissed loudly as it moved more quickly. "No, Marcellus, no," it said with urgency. "That is precisely why they are a threat. Can a strong Empire last through weakness and cowardice? Can your children's Empire resist the Sassanids, Armenians, and Germans if its soldiers and citizens do not sacrifice to the gods?"

Marcellus thought for a moment. "Some of my best soldiers are Christians."

"Can you not see what Galerius and Diocletian see?" said the dragon as it hissed out a long stream of smoke. "They love the Empire and look far into its future. If the best and noblest – like your Christian soldiers – are confused about their masters, what does that say about everyone else? Think, Marcellus, think. If the Germans became Christians, would Christian soldiers fight at the western frontiers? Who would protect us?"

The thought sunk heavily into Marcellus.

"Is there really so much at stake?" he wondered out loud.

The dragon continued as if Marcellus hadn't spoken. "Lucius understands, just like Galerius and Diocletian. No Christians on his estate, and slaves are kept in their place. The Empire, Marcellus. Think of the Empire."

Marcellus looked down as his thoughts raced. "What do you want from me?"

"Only two things, Marcellus," said the dragon as it flicked its tail and again wrapped itself around Marcellus. "After all, one man – even a good man like you – can only do so much. Abolish these Christians from your estate. And bring me a sacrifice."

Marcellus looked up. "I cannot do the first. It is still my father's estate, and I will not work against his wishes."

"Of course, Marcellus, of course," said the dragon soothingly. "But you can talk to him. I know that he does not believe in me yet. Why not tell him about me? I am patient, Marcellus, very patient."

"Very well. But again, my father only sacrifices to his ancestors and the Roman gods."

"I know. He is such a good man. Tell me: what happens to the meat from a sacrifice to the gods?"

"It is eaten, of course."

"Look at me, Marcellus. Unlike the gods, I need to eat. So think of it as an offering to a friend. And we have so much to talk about, so come in two days with something – a few sheep or goats will do."

"How can you be older than the gods but still have a body?"

The dragon chuckled again. "Do you really know so much about the gods, Marcellus? Or about creatures like me? Does anyone? The Christians are silly and foolish when they say they know all about the gods. Now go to your father's house. You have a wedding to prepare, and you must come see me in two days."

Marcellus turned to go, but stopped as a thought occurred to him. "What is the Empire for, dragon? How do we know it is so important?"

The dragon hissed again, but there was no hint of anger in its voice. "Think of Cicero, Marcellus. Did he not devote his whole life to the glory of Rome? His every word was aimed at the improvement of Roman citizens and Roman government. And yet he never answered such a question. Can anyone? The brave and noble men are the ones who do what is right for their Empire and their families even without answers to such questions."

Marcellus could not reply. The dragon broke the short silence. "It is getting late, Marcellus. Go back to your father's estate and arrange a sacrifice for me."

Briefly, Marcellus wondered if he should. Then he looked at the dragon's red eyes and felt strengthened. He saw an uncontrolled, fiery force in them, but they also seemed to contain his ambitions: marriage to Regina, a glorious career in the army, and the life of a noble and wealthy Roman citizen. As he breathed in deeply, he also noticed that the dragon had been right: he was getting used to the smell.

He made his decision. "I will go back and arrange a sacrifice," he responded.

CHAPTER SEVEN

A STRANGE GATHERING

Until he got to the old shed, Marcellus was wrapped up in his own thoughts.

He thought about the sacrifice he would bring to the dragon, and he wondered how he would get it to the dragon's cave. He wondered what, if anything, he would say to his father about the dragon. He thought about Regina and his wedding in nine days. He thought about the Empire and the army and all that they meant to him. Once, he asked himself the last question he had asked the dragon: What was the Empire for? But mostly, he thought about the dragon.

He remembered the eyes. More than once, he looked into the ruby eyes on his armband to try to feel like he was with the dragon. The light reflected in the rubies dimly suggested a fire behind them, but they only made Marcellus long for the real thing. Why did he want to dive into those eyes? Why did he want to give himself – actually, lose himself – in the dragon-life behind those eyes? And why was there a part of him that was repulsed by such an idea? He did not know.

The singing from the old shed drew his attention away from these thoughts. The voices were clear and strong and happy at first. Then came some low chanting by a single voice, then a chorus again, this time clear and strong and somewhat melancholy. Then chanting again, then a happier chorus. Without Marcellus' prompting, Kopto moved toward the shed.

As Kopto walked slowly toward the singing, Marcellus was able to make out some of the words. He heard "Lord, have mercy" repeatedly and a longer song about "the cross of life that destroyed death." The lone voice chanted "Father, Son, and Holy Spirit" several times and intoned longer sets of words that could not be heard clearly.

The singing and chanting attracted Marcellus, but he did not know why. He had heard music like it at temples dedicated to Roman gods, but nothing quite so earnest, happy, sorrowful, and hopeful all at the same time. And he had never heard men and women singing together.

"Whoa, Kopto." The horse's nose was almost inside the shed. Marcellus dismounted and looked in.

About two dozen people faced away from him. They were bathed in golden light from candles placed around the perimeter. At the far end of the shed was a small, crude table. In front of the table, also facing away from him, was a man in some kind of a light-colored robe who was separated from the rest of the people.

He must be some kind of priest, thought Marcellus.

The singing stopped and the man in the light-colored robe turned around. He was about to speak when he noticed Marcellus. His eyes widened, causing the rest of the people to turn to the door. A short commotion ensued as they realized who was looking in. Embarrassed, Marcellus drew back.

A voice – Marcellus guessed that it was the priest's – chanted, "May Christ our true God, through the prayers of the martyrs..." Marcellus did not recognize the names that followed, and he was too occupied with his own embarrassment and puzzlement to listen to the rest. When the people had looked at him, he was startled to see slaves and free men in the same place, even standing side by side. Also to his surprise were the men and women standing next to

"The singing and chanting attracted Marcellus, but he did not know why."

each other. He had never heard of worship where men and women were not separated in some way. Among the slaves were foreign soldiers he had captured along with some born on the estate. Some farmers who lived near his father's estate were there with their wives and children. He did not know for sure, but he felt that there were some faces he did not know, and he certainly had never seen the robed man before.

The singing had stopped, and the people began to come out of the door. Those Marcellus did not know passed an embarrassed glance in his direction. Those who were from his father's estate quickly bowed to him, and one slave even knelt down and kissed his hand. A few lingered and spoke with each other, but most walked away quickly. No doubt, thought Marcellus, to beat the coming darkness. The farmers bowed to him and mounted the horses he had noticed before.

"Master!" By the time Marcellus looked in the direction of the voice, Pasikrates was kneeling before him with his head bowed.

Marcellus smiled. "Stand up, Pasikrates, and tell me what is going on here."

Pasikrates spoke excitedly as he rose. "The bishop is here, Master! All with your father's permission, of course. All the Christians from the estate are here – well, most of them." He looked up. "Let me see, Eurymathos is sick, and Claudius is with him, and Helena – she is a slave in the kitchens – was too tired to come out for vespers – which is evening prayer. I know we're missing a few others, but I just cannot think right now. But the bishop! You must meet him!"

Before Marcellus could respond, the robed man appeared in the doorway. When he saw Marcellus, he immediately walked over, bowed, and looked Marcellus in the eye. His eyes were almost royal blue and edged with a soft, inviting expression. Like an ocean on a calm day, thought Marcellus. He took a deep breath.

Then the man said, "I knew you would be coming."

CHAPTER EIGHT

A NIGHTTIME CONVERSATION

S tartled, Marcellus broke his gaze, but then quickly looked back into the man's eyes.

"How could you know that?" he asked.

Without hesitation, the man answered, "Two weeks ago, while praying, I had a vision. I was in a field, facing the setting sun. I saw a man running toward me – not frantically, but steadily. Behind him was a scaly, serpent-like beast. The man – it was you – stopped in front of me. The beast moved in behind the man. And then I woke up."

Marcellus looked down to hide the confusion in his mind. Who is this man? he wondered anxiously. How does he know about the dragon? What do I say?   Pasikrates intervened. "Master, this is Agathon, our priest – actually, our bishop. Your father has been good enough to let him stay with me when he visits. Your good father also lets us use this old shed for our prayers."

Marcellus looked back up, and Agathon bowed to him. Marcellus bowed back.

"Do such dreams come to you often, Agathon?"

Again without hesitation, Agathon replied, "Almost never. I have been a Christian nearly twenty years and this is only the second time the Lord has spoken to me in a dream."

"What was the first one about?"

Agathon smiled and pointed to the sunset. "If we wait much longer, our horses will stumble through the dark."

Marcellus nodded and mounted Kopto. "I will ride ahead and prepare some food. Pasikrates, bring Agathon to my rooms when you are done here."

As he rode toward the estate, Marcellus felt grateful for some time alone before he met with Agathon. From his negotiations with enemy commanders, he had learned that time was usually his friend. It allowed him to assess the situation, quell passions like anger and pride, and organize soldiers in case negotiations broke down.

At this moment, Marcellus was full of passions, some of them in competition with one another. He was confused. How did Agathon dream about the dragon, and what did it mean? Was he a messenger from the gods or, perhaps, the strange Christian god? He felt fear – not the fear of a soldier in battle, but the fear of powers he was unable to control. He was also offended by what he had just seen: slaves, men, women, wealthy farmers and poor servants singing together. Such a gathering was against all of the unspoken rules for Roman society.

And the dragon was still in his mind. Even without closing his eyes, he could smell the stale air from the cave and feel the trembling in his body when he first saw the dragon. And then the blood-red eyes and his desire to lose part of himself – or all of himself – in them. And there was his desire to please Regina. She had lost herself in the dragon, it seemed, and would it not be wise to follow her? After all, the dragon had only asked for a few sheep, something his father's estate would not miss.

After dispatching a slave to fix some food and wine, Marcellus changed into a comfortable robe and arranged cushions around a low table. The slave returned with olives, bread, cheese, and two pitchers of wine right before Pasikrates and Agathon entered the room.

Pasikrates bowed immediately. "Is there anything else I can get, master?"

"No, Pasikrates. Wait outside. When Agathon and I are done talking, you can escort him back to your quarters. Why not send that other slave to bed? If we need anything, I will call on you."

Pasikrates bowed again. He was about to leave the room when Agathon said, "I was hoping Pasikrates would join us."

Marcellus was so surprised that he answered without thinking, "But he is a slave!"

"In your eyes and according to Roman law, yes. But in God's eyes he is a man, an equal. And given the amount of affection he bears for you and your father, he is a friend."

Marcellus looked at Pasikrates who, red-faced, seemed surprised as well. Agathon noticed, too, and quickly added, "My apologies, Marcellus and Pasikrates. I have offended you both. Pasikrates, disregard what I said and listen to your master, as you are accustomed."

Pasikrates bowed and left the room quickly.

Agathon turned to Marcellus and bowed. "Again, I am sorry to make you so uncomfortable."

When Marcellus looked at the sea-blue eyes, he could tell that Agathon meant what he said. But behind the eyes, it seemed, was a gentle vision that eluded him.

Not knowing what to say, Marcellus waved his hand toward the table. "Please enjoy some food and wine with me."

Agathon nodded and sat down. As they began eating, Agathon said, "You must tell me, Marcellus, if my dream has any meaning to you. Our holy writings say that we must test every spirit, and I know that demons can speak in dreams like God."

Feeling cautious, Marcellus responded, "I like this idea of testing, so let me test you first."

"Very well," laughed Agathon as he drank some wine. "I am the guest, after all. What would you like to know?"

"I would like to know how you came to be leading a band of Christians on my father's estate."

Agathon relaxed into some cushions with his goblet of wine. "I will have to go back to my beginning. I presume you have time."

Marcellus pointed to the table. "Time and food and wine for many hours."

Marcellus had no difficulty understanding the first part of Agathon's story. He was the second son of a provincial Roman governor, so he grew up with slaves, wealth, and an access to books that made Marcellus think of the library in Lucius' villa. When Agathon said, "not many days go by when Cicero does not come into my mind," Marcellus nodded appreciatively.

Agathon's mother was a Christian, and while his father did not allow his children to be baptized, he did not stop his wife, along with the tutors who were Christians, from educating the children in the Christian holy writings and dogmas. He had been ready to study law and rhetoric in Alexandria when his father died and his older brother began managing the family estate.

"I love my brother," said Agathon with a sigh, "but he quickly became hard and cruel. Unlike me, he had always preferred competing and ruling over learning and books. That is why he always disliked Christian teachings. He married our two younger sisters off to other hard and cruel men, ignoring my complaints and my mother's protests. He also refused to give me the gold I needed to finish my studies. One evening, after visiting with my mother, I returned to my quarters and found my slave dead next to a goblet of empty wine. He had been poisoned, and I knew that the poison had been meant for me. I quickly returned to my mother. She gave me the few coins she had, and I fled."

Marcellus had heard similar stories from his soldiers. Unable to receive anything from their father or exiled from their families, they joined the Roman army. But he found it hard to relate to the rest of Agathon's story.

"I went to Aristarchus, my mother's bishop," continued Agathon. "He took me in, saying he was repaying my mother for all of her donations over the years. But there were others there who were far poorer than I was. Some were, like me, fleeing family, and many were fleeing persecution from Roman authorities. Most were Christians, of course, but not all.

"I had never been with so many Christians before, nor had I ever met Christians who had suffered for their faith. Many more arrived after me, and Aristarchus somehow made room for them all, even the women and the slaves. And that was another thing: I had never lived without slaves. There, the slaves were not slaves. All shared in the tasks of the estate. I and others highly born did slave's work, yet we did it willingly, even cheerfully. Those who were weak and sick did less, those who were young and strong did more. Even Aristarchus did slave's work when he was not traveling to one of his churches."

Agathon went on to explain how the words of his Christian education began to make sense as he watched these people pray and work together. People who arrived were welcomed, and people who left went to a secure position, usually arranged by Aristarchus.

"A desire to become a Christian grew steadily in me," Agathon continued. "One day, I approached Aristarchus and asked for baptism. 'You are not ready,' said Aristarchus. 'But why?' I asked. Then Aristarchus did something unusual – unusual, at least, to my mind at the time. He put his right hand on my head and prayed, 'O Lord Jesus Christ, who alone loves mankind, reveal yourself and your Holy Spirit to your servant Agathon. Lead him to worship you in spirit and in truth. For yours is the kingdom and the glory, together with the Father and the Holy Spirit, now and ever and unto ages of ages. Amen.'"

Agathon paused. "He was right, of course. I was not ready. I admired and loved the goodness of Aristarchus and the community around him, but I did not really know its source. As Aristarchus put it later, I loved the warm rays but not the sun."

Agathon paused, looking away and smiling slightly. He breathed in deeply.

"So what happened?" asked Marcellus.

Agathon looked at Marcellus. Again, a powerful but gentle happiness resided in Agathon's sea-blue eyes.

"What happened? I found the sun. No, that is not right. The sun found me – but that is not quite right either. I do not fully understand it. I came to know, and I am coming to know, the source of that goodness. And he did not reject me, so I want nothing more than to lose myself and find myself in him. Have you ever felt that way?"

Although startled by the question, Marcellus answered, "Yes," thinking of the dragon.

"Perhaps you will tell me about it," continued Agathon, "but I must finish my story and answer your question. Aristarchus noticed that I was educated, so he prepared me to become a priest even as I prepared to be baptized. I had no wish to marry – I did not have any money or land, after all – so after serving as a priest for four years, he recommended that I become a bishop. The other bishops agreed with him, so I was made a bishop and assigned to this region. I heard that your mother was a Christian, so I suspected that your father was at least sympathetic to my faith. He was. He even had some slaves repair that old shed. And that," he said as he picked up his goblet, "is why I am here leading Christians in prayer."

"But you are not afraid of getting caught? You must have heard about Diocletian and Galerius and the persecutions."

"What if I am caught? What if I am brought before Diocletian himself? I will die, that is all. I am going to die sometime anyway, and the promise of our God is that his children will be raised to live with him forever. But I am careful – I do not go looking for death. I stay mostly with fellow Christians or on estates like this one."

Marcellus was silent. He had never heard a man speak so simply and confidently about death. Vague stories about an afterlife were often heard prior to battles and raids, and Marcellus' memory was full of Greek and Roman stories about souls in torment or paradise after death. Cicero, he remembered, wrote confidently about pure and devout men going to live with the gods. Marcellus' experience, though, had taught him that death was bearable for soldiers only because dishonor was unbearable. No soldier wanted to live with the label "coward," so they quickly learned to face danger and death.

"Marcellus?"

Marcellus looked into Agathon's eyes again. There, alongside a peace that Marcellus could not fathom, was friendship. At that moment, Marcellus realized that he did not know what to do about the dragon, and thus he needed a friend. He made a decision.

"Your dream – it was accurate, I think," he said slowly. "At least the part about the beast. Since the gods – or your god – gave you this dream, perhaps you can help me understand this beast."

Agathon was clearly surprised, but leaned back on his pillows and said, "I will listen. I may not have much wisdom to share, however."

"I woke up this morning at my fiancée's estate," Marcellus began. He told Agathon about Regina's plea for him to see the dragon, the story of Regina's slave, the trip to see the dragon, and then, with some difficulty, the details of his encounter with the dragon itself.

When Marcellus finished, he took off his armband and handed it to Agathon. Agathon's face darkened as he fingered it. He handed the armband back to Marcellus and, to Marcellus' surprise, stood up and began pacing.

"I have heard of such beasts," he said without looking at Marcellus, "but I did not know they existed."

"What is this beast, Agathon? What have you heard?"

"This beast is a liar. It is a descendant of the father of lies." Agathon was about to say something else, but sat down in silence. Then he looked at Marcellus. "You exposed its lie, or one of them. 'What is the purpose of the empire?' That was an excellent question, Marcellus. This beast loves nothing, cares for nothing, lives for nothing."

Marcellus frowned. He was surprised by Agathon's boldness. After all, Agathon was simply a guest. Marcellus was also worried. He had promised the dragon some sheep, and his future wife certainly favored the dragon more than Christians. When he looked back into Agathon's eyes, however, he again felt a desire for his help and friendship.

"Are you saying that I should not provide this dragon with anything?" asked Marcellus.

"Would you feed a wild dog that wanted to bite you?"

"But he loves the empire."

"It lies. It has no love for the empire or for you or for anyone else. It does not even love itself."

"What should I do, then?"

"I can only tell you what I would do. I would do nothing. I would not offer sacrifice to this beast, and I would not go back to see it. I would also pray."

"But what about Regina?"

57

"Christians try to do the right thing no matter the consequences. Many times the outcome is something better than we could have expected."

"And many times, the outcome is death. Senseless death, it seems."

"Yes, sometimes it is death. If Galerius has his way, the outcome will often be death. But death for the sake of the Lord, or even for the sake of what is right, is never senseless."

Marcellus shook his head. Suddenly, he felt exhausted. "I do not know, Agathon. I am afraid it is time to retire. Perhaps we can speak more tomorrow."

Agathon rose respectfully. "I am sorry, Marcellus, but I will be traveling tomorrow. I will be back here in four or five days. We can speak then. Please know that I am very grateful for the food and for the bed."

Agathon bowed, and Marcellus bowed in return. After Agathon roused a sleeping Pasikrates in the hallway, Marcellus went to his bedroom, undressed, and tried to sleep.

When he closed his eyes, however, he fell into the red eyes of the dragon, cast Christians off his father's estate, and watched the dragon consume his sheep. Startled, he opened his eyes and paced in his room until his heartbeat slowed. When he closed his eyes again, he fell into Agathon's sea-blue eyes, singing with slaves and feeling the wrath of the dragon at a distance. Startled, he opened his eyes and paced again.

And so he fitfully dozed and paced until he said to himself, "I will not sacrifice to the dragon." He did not know why he said it, but he felt some relief. Then he slid into a continuous but uneasy sleep.

CHAPTER NINE

WEDDING PREPARATIONS AND A DREAM

For the next two days, Marcellus allowed himself to be consumed with the details of the upcoming wedding. He checked the stores of wine and food, saw that rooms were prepared for guests, and assigned the slaves special duties. He directed some artisans to decorate his room with a new mural of Venus, the goddess of love, as a gift for Regina.

Pasikrates was unusually cheerful and helpful. He was obviously pleased that his master was getting married. But Marcellus suspected that he was even more pleased that his master and Agathon had enjoyed each other's company. He did not react negatively to Agathon's departure.

"He will be back soon, and we Christians can pray without him," Pasikrates said with a smile. "Is there more work you would like me to do, master?"

Marcellus was pleased, especially when he realized that Pasikrates continued to manage the estate while carrying out all these extra tasks. Once, when Pasikrates was walking to a large room that was being transformed into a banqueting hall, Marcellus saw him dispatch three slaves to various tasks around the estate, answer questions of three others, and help two other slaves carry tools for measuring the room.

The only time Marcellus thought of the dragon was when he received a short letter from Regina before an evening meal. Pasikrates brought it to him, accompanied by two slaves carrying large jugs of wine.

"From the future lady of this house," announced Pasikrates as he handed a small parchment to Marcellus. "And this wine came with it."

As Marcellus opened the parchment, he recognized Regina's handwriting. It was like her: bold and clear, yet still soft and pleasing to the eye. The letter read,

My Dear Marcellus,

As I long for our wedding day, so I long to know of your meeting with the dragon. I would go to the dragon myself, but I am ferociously busy with the wedding – much like you, I know. I sent a slave to the dragon with a sacrifice of two cows and a pig. I am sure that the dragon will be pleased. I coaxed father into digging out two jugs of his best wine for the wedding. Consider it a sacrifice for you, my dear. Until then, look at your armband and think of me.

Regina

Marcellus looked at his armband, thought of Regina, and felt guilty. How could he explain his decision to not sacrifice to the dragon when he did not understand it himself? He had no more than a hunch that Agathon was right. Perhaps, he thought, I will write to her tomorrow.

Pasikrates placed a goblet of wine in Marcellus' free hand. "A sample of the jugs from Lucius. You should go to bed soon, master. Leave the details of the wedding to me."

Marcellus sipped the wine and sighed. "I will go to bed after I eat and bathe. But in the morning, we will meet right after you talk with my father. In the army, I learned to never leave all the details to someone else – not even a trusted slave."

Pasikrates smiled at the compliment and nodded. "As you wish, master."

This is good wine, thought Marcellus as Pasikrates walked off to give orders to two other slaves. He drained the goblet, ate his meal, relaxed in a hot bath, and contentedly climbed into his bed. It occurred to him again that he would have to explain to Regina why there was no sacrifice for the dragon. But sleep overtook him before he could give any thought to the matter.

Later, he figured that he must have started dreaming quite a while after he fell asleep, for the sun rose not long after he woke up.

The dream began pleasantly. Marcellus sat comfortably on an island beach, feeling the warmth of the sun through a light tunic. Waves rolled gently up to his feet, which were partially buried in warm sand. Beside him was a bowl of grapes and a plate with bread and cheese. He ate slowly and contentedly. He presumed that there were slaves available to meet all of his needs and desires, even though he couldn't see them.

He reached to the plate for some cheese, but felt it move under his fingers. When he looked down, he noticed a small crack in the sand underneath the plate. How had he missed it before? Then he noticed that the fissure was getting bigger. Before he could move the plate, it fell down the widening hole which, he thought, would soon engulf him.

When he stood up, he saw not one or two, but several fissures spreading like jagged lightning across the ground. He ran along the beach to escape the fissure closest to him, only to be cut off by a new crack in front of him. He turned toward the center of the island, but saw another fissure in that direction which was too wide to cross. The island was breaking up.

Frightened, Marcellus turned to the sea. A boat sailed some ways from the shore. Several people were on it, singing like the Christians in the old shed. Somehow, Marcellus knew that they were slaves – probably the slaves that he expected to be tending to him. Marcellus also knew that he was not a good swimmer, but soon he would be forced into the water by the fissuring island. He wanted to jump into the water and ask for help, but he felt paralyzed – perhaps by fear, perhaps by shame for asking slaves for any kind of help.

Suddenly, Marcellus was in a field on his father's estate. There was no wind, and the sun glared in his eyes and beat down on him oppressively. Then he heard laughter coming from the sky. He looked up. There, circling like an eagle, was the dragon.

More laughter. This time, he recognized it. It was Demetrios' laugh, filling the inside of his tent. Then it changed into the silvery laughter of Regina as she secretly visited Marcellus in the night. Then came the quiet chuckle of his father over a goblet of wine. Then the riotous laughter of the revelers at Lucius' estate. Then the dragon's deep, sneering chuckle.

The dragon began flying toward him. Again, he heard the different laughs. As the dragon flew closer, they became louder and more jumbled. Marcellus tried to put his hands over his ears, but he could not move. The laughs became louder and more jumbled still, combining into a deafening, mocking cackle coming from the dragon's mouth. The dragon's eyes glowed, intent upon devouring Marcellus. He knew he could not stop it. With his head and body rumbling from the roar, he resigned himself to fate and watched the massive teeth descend upon him.

Then, Marcellus woke up. But the roar did not stop. A human voice cried in the distance. He could smell smoke and see the glow of a nearby fire through his window. More cries came from a distance. As the roar receded slightly, Marcellus realized what was happening. The dragon was attacking the estate.

CHAPTER TEN

AN ATTACK

When he first ran out into the courtyard, Marcellus saw three fires close by and one in the distance. The firelight illumined dozens of people running about chaotically. Some were hauling sloshing buckets to one of the fires, and a few were carrying motionless bodies away from flames. Most, however, did not seem to be running anywhere in particular.

Marcellus coughed. The air was thick with smoke. I must find Pasikrates, he thought as he continued to cough.

"Master!"

Marcellus turned around. Pasikrates stood before him, his alarmed face blackened and his panicky eyes bloodshot.

"Master, some creature – I cannot tell what it is. It flies and spews fire. And it – oh, I still do not know if I saw it do this – but I think it may have eaten a slave!" He choked and wiped his eyes. "I sent a few people to rescue those in burning buildings, especially the children. But you must help, master! Quickly! Before you lose everything!"

Seeing Pasikrates jolted Marcellus' memory. "What about my father?"

"He is –" Pasikrates coughed and wiped his eyes again. "He is –"

At that moment, several things happened at once. Not far above Marcellus' head, a deafening roar split the air, accompanied by a rush of foul air and a crashing sound from a nearby roof.

Marcellus instinctively covered his ears and bent down as he felt his stomach churn from the rotten stench in the air. When he looked up, Pasikrates was gone. He glanced at the roof and saw fire-light reflected in thousands of scales moving about with chaotic rhythm. The dragon was tearing tiles off the roof with its claws. Its tail thrashed repeatedly, sending other tiles flying into the court-yard. Then he saw the darkly glittering form of the dragon creep to the edge of the roof and leap down into the courtyard. It turned and shot fire out of its mouth at a wooden beam supporting the roof. Almost instantly, the beam was aflame. Then the dragon flew off.

As he heard cries and smelled the smoke and the dragon's stench, Marcellus grabbed a nearby stone, hurled it, and screamed in anger while running in the direction of the dragon's flight. He imagined himself hacking the dragon's limbs off with his sword and plunging a spear into its long, sinewy body.

Think like a soldier! he told himself as the dragon disappeared from his sight. He knew that he could not fight the dragon at night, so he resolved to try to organize the people on the estate to put out fires and get others to safety.

"Pasikrates!" he yelled.

There was no response. He saw a pair of slaves running away from a flaming building with buckets in their hands. He hurried to them. When they saw him, they bowed quickly.

"Are there others who can help you?" shouted Marcellus above the cries and sound of the flames.

"A few already have, but they disappeared when the beast re-turned," answered one slave. "We cannot keep track of many peo-ple, and it is enough to keep ourselves safe!"

Marcellus nodded. "Every time you find someone who can car-ry water, bring them with you. Stay away from the courtyard – it is too easy to get attacked there, and you might get hit with tiles from the roof. Try to put out one fire at a time. It is easier to rebuild a few structures than to repair them all." Marcellus looked at the sky

"The dragon was tearing tiles off the roof with its claws."

and noticed, through the smoke, that clouds covered the moon and stars. "If people cannot help you, send them into the fields where it is dark, and tell them to stick together and wait for someone to get them when the sun rises."

The two slaves quickly bowed and ran off. Marcellus spied another slave on the other side of the courtyard. He yelled, but his voice did not carry through the flames and the cries. He looked in the sky for the dragon. When he did not see it, he decided to risk a run across the courtyard.

When he got to the middle of the courtyard, the dragon descended with a thunderous crackle. Marcellus fell on the ground, covering his ears. A wave of foul air passed over him, causing him to retch. When he was able to get up, he turned and saw the dragon through the smoke. It was looking at him. In front of it were two mangled, bloody, and lifeless sheep. The dragon dug its claws into one, ripping it into two pieces. Then it ate each piece ravenously. The dragon did the same with the second sheep, eyeing Marcellus the entire time. The dragon flicked its tail, sending stones and tiles flying around the courtyard. It screeched again as it flew off above the buildings of the estate.

Breathing heavily, Marcellus stumbled to the edge of the courtyard. He fell once before he got to a building.

Think like a soldier, he told himself again.

He slowly began to look for others. As he found them, he sent them to put out fires or go into the fields. To his relief, the dragon did not attack again that night.

CHAPTER ELEVEN

THE DRAGON, AGAIN

The extent of the dragon's attack became visible at dawn. Half of the slaves' quarters had been burnt. Debris from several roofs lay everywhere. Smoke came from so many places that it seemed as if a fog was lifting off the estate. Marcellus had counted three dead bodies, but feared there were more. He guessed that the dragon had killed more sheep than the two he had seen, and he presumed that some crops had been burnt. Given what the dragon had said about Christians, he also guessed that the old shed had been destroyed.

As Marcellus looked around, his mind smoldered like the buildings around him. The feeling was not new to him. At some point in almost all of his battles and raids, raw rage had swelled up inside him. Sometimes, it came from seeing a comrade die, and sometimes it grew from the thought of foreign powers ruling over Romans. Sometimes it was simply a reaction to the audacity of foreigners crossing clearly established Roman borders.

Marcellus knew that such passion was dangerous. He had seen many men, both foreign and Roman, lose their minds to rage and become reckless. Such recklessness usually led to their deaths.

Occasionally, it led to the defeat of an entire army. But he also knew that it was valuable. Without it, soldiers would give into their fear too easily and hasten disastrous defeats.

As he smoldered, Marcellus thought of Regina. "What will she think of this?" he wondered aloud. But mostly, he thought about the dragon. The blood-red eyes that had entranced him now stirred vengeance in his heart. He could only think of the strong, sinewy body as the object of blows from his sword. As he smelled the remnants of the dragon's stench, his desire to ride Kopto to the dragon increased.

Suddenly, through a crowd of people returning from the fields, Pasikrates ran to Marcellus, breathing heavily. His face and clothes were streaked with soot. "Master," he panted, "you must come see your father."

* * *

When he first walked into his father's room, Marcellus felt relief. "He is awake!" he exclaimed.

Then he noticed. His father's eyes seemed fixated on a point beyond the ceiling. They did not move, and they blinked only a few times. His father's mouth was open slightly, as if frozen in surprise.

"I found him like this," said Pasikrates, "and I found you as soon as I could."

As Marcellus stared at his father, he clenched his teeth and tightened his fists. "Leave me alone for a moment."

"Master, I will stay – "

"Leave me!" yelled Marcellus.

Pasikrates hurried out.

Marcellus took deep breaths, trying to control the rising tide of emotion in his heart. He closed his eyes and tried to clear his mind, but in rapid succession, he saw his father showing him how to hold a shield, his father looking over crops with Pasikrates, and his father smiling next to his mother at a meal.

Something like a ball of blackness formed inside him. Then it grew so that he was forced to fall on his knees while letting out a sound between a sob and a yell. He knelt on the floor like that, his hand on his father's arm, alternately weeping and trying to catch his breath.

Soon, he was able to take a deep breath again. There will be no sacrifices to this dragon, he thought. The dragon itself will be a sacrifice.

* * *

After hastily putting on some armor and securing a spear, his sword, and a shield, Marcellus rode Kopto hard through Lucius' estate. He did not stop to acknowledge the surprised looks and waves from the slaves and workers in the fields. He stopped and rested Kopto at a small pond near the edge of Lucius' estate, then rode steadily past the hills, trees, and increasingly lifeless landscape to the top of the cliff and down the rocky path. Kopto must have sensed Marcellus' anger and determination, for the horse did not resist as it neared the cave.

Marcellus sat quietly on Kopto outside the dragon's cave, Kopto hoofed the ground nervously.. The lifeless stench in and around the cave had dampened Marcellus' anger. He again felt the dread that was in the air near the dragon. Still, his anger and desire for revenge were strong.

"Dragon!" he yelled at the cave. "Show yourself!"

A short time passed. Marcellus was about to yell again when he saw the yellow talons at the edge of the cave. He grabbed his spear and held it back, ready to throw.

"Marcellus," came the dragon's smooth, undisturbed voice. "My dear Marcellus, put that spear down."

Marcellus shook his head and shouted again, "Show yourself!"

The talons moved forward. Marcellus could see the dim, red flicker of the dragon's eyes.

"Marcellus," came the dragon's voice again, "why are you so angry? You promised to bring me two sheep. I simply took them when you did not come. You have lost nothing."

Marcellus' right hand relaxed. Was the dragon right? He had agreed to bring the dragon something to eat. And I want to please Regina, he thought, so perhaps I should leave the dragon alone. Maybe I should bring him more sheep tomorrow.

Then he remembered his father's vacant eyes. He remembered the dead slaves, the smoldering buildings on his estate, and the soot on Pasikrates' face. He remembered Agathon's words: "The dragon is a liar."

Unable to control his anger, Marcellus gripped his spear and spurred Kopto's side. Kopto, however, was unwilling to move and reared up. While gripping Kopto's reigns, Marcellus saw the dragon dart out of the cave. Marcellus hurled the spear across his body as Kopto landed, but it sailed over the dragon's tail. Madly, Marcellus pulled Kopto's reins to turn the horse toward the dragon. Before he was all the way around, he saw the dragon's tail sweep toward Kopto's legs. Kopto reared up again, but the tail hit his back legs. Marcellus instinctively released the reins and fell off in the direction opposite the dragon, grabbing his sword hilt to guide his fall.

Miraculously, Marcellus landed with the sword in his hands. The dragon made a half-charge at Kopto, forcing the horse to run away. Then it turned its red eyes toward Marcellus. Marcellus clambered to his feet, holding his sword in both hands.

It seemed to Marcellus that as the dragon moved closer, it was smiling to itself. It was as if the dragon was a cat and Marcellus a mouse with no escape. But his soldierly instincts had taken over, and he was ready to fight even in the face of certain death.

The dragon stopped. Marcellus stood still, ready to move in any direction, his eyes fixed on the dragon. The dragon snorted heavily, letting a nebulous ball of smoke out of its mouth. A reeking, sulfuric smell reached Marcellus, and he could not stop himself from retching.

The dragon pounced. Marcellus raised his sword, but he could not hold onto it when the dragon's talons crashed against his arm. Somehow, he was able to stand up after the blow, and he saw his sword in the dragon's teeth. With its red eyes locked on Marcellus, the dragon jerked its head. The sword flew through the air away from Marcellus. Again, the dragon prowled forward with a smiling look on its face.

Marcellus backed up and looked for an escape. There was none. The dragon inched closer. Suddenly, it lunged forward and spun around at the same time. The dragon hurled its tail at Marcellus' feet. Marcellus crashed to the ground. He expected the dragon to jump on him at that moment. Instead, he was able to scramble to his feet. The dragon moved forward. At that moment, Marcellus felt his life drain from him. He sat down, then lay down, waiting for the dragon to devour him.

Instantly, the dragon was on top of him, pinning his arms with its talons. Crushing pain rippled through his arms and shoulders. His legs were immobile under the dragon's belly. The dragon brought its head close to Marcellus' face. Again, Marcellus smelled the reek of the dragon's breath. He felt his stomach turn just before he lost consciousness.

* * *

When Marcellus opened his eyes, the sun was high in the sky. His face was hot and his body was stiff. His head ached. He tried to get up, but an unsettled feeling in his stomach and a spinning feeling in his head forced him to lie back down.

After gliding in and out of consciousness a few times, he was able to sit up. He looked for Kopto, but saw only the dragon. It was looking at him with its deep, blood-red eyes.

"Hello, Marcellus," said the dragon. Marcellus again thought he detected a faint smile.

"Why have you not killed me?" Marcellus demanded weakly.

The dragon snorted. "I mean you no harm, Marcellus. Why can you not see that? Those Christians on your estate" – Marcellus heard a hiss again – "like to talk about a God of mercy, but I am the one who has shown you mercy. Your horse is well and you are alive. I even recovered your sword for you."

Marcellus tried to stand up, but his head started to spin again. From his knees, he said, "Why have you done this?"

"My dear soldier," said the dragon as it crept closer to Marcellus, "I want to be your friend. Look at me."

Marcellus was unable to resist. When his eyes met the dragon's, he felt relief and foolishness. He was relieved of his hate for the dragon, and he felt foolish for doubting its words and trusting Agathon. Was it not obvious that the dragon wanted to be his friend? The dragon had his best interest in mind – his marriage, his estate, his beloved empire. And was it not reasonable for it to ask for a little food?

"Stand up now," said the dragon.

Marcellus obeyed.

"Now, Marcellus, I need a sacrifice from you. Three sheep, or something like that. Come back with them in three days. Set out plenty early, for we know that sheep are not the fastest creatures on land."

Marcellus nodded. The dragon had not released him from its gaze. He was feeling stronger and less dizzy. A voice in his head warned him about the dragon, and scenes from his dream flashed into his mind, but they were easy to ignore when he was surrendering to the dragon's eyes. "I will be back in three days," he said quietly.

The dragon swished its tail and circled Marcellus on its way back to its cave. "Go home now, Marcellus," it said, "and do not forget your sword."

Marcellus obeyed.

CHAPTER TWELVE

ANOTHER MEETING
WITH REGINA

Although the sun shone brightly and a light, refreshing breeze wafted through the villa, Marcellus felt nothing but dullness as he went about his routines the next day. He mechanically ate his bread and cheese while a shaken Pasikrates related all the happenings on the estate. He nodded mechanically as Pasikrates talked, and he simply agreed with all of Pasikrates' suggestions. When Pasikrates mentioned that Agathon was returning that day, Marcellus had to be reminded of who Agathon was.

When he visited his still unresponsive father, he felt only some of the anger and sadness of the previous day. Perhaps this is my doing, he thought. Perhaps the dragon is right. A few sheep – a little bit of food – and my father would still be with me.

As Marcellus stared at his father, watching his chest gently rise and fall, he again saw images of his father as an active, happy man. And again, he wept, although this time in a soft rhythm that mirrored his father's breaths. He saw the dragon's deep red eyes in his mind, and as he surrendered to them, he murmured to himself, "My father will die soon, and I will have to manage the estate for him."

Marcellus tried to alter his inner dullness with work. He repeatedly threw a spear at a target. He undertook combat drills with his sword and shield. To the surprise of his slaves, he even helped clear some of the debris in the courtyard.

All of these activities, however, only reminded him of the dragon's attack and his inability to avenge himself and his father. Every time he thought of resisting the dragon's will, a glance at the charred buildings and broken roof tiles prevented that from becoming a desire. Resisting the dragon, he thought, would be like fighting an army of 8,000 with 800 men.

A few times, he tried to use Cicero to dispel his mood. Without knowing why, he remembered a passage about grieving: "Weeping much over a friend's death shows how much you love yourself, not your friend." This caused him to think about his father, however, and any rising spirit was quickly lowered. He recalled some passages about suffering and character, and he remembered Cicero's many words about the glory of the Roman Republic. But this only reminded him that the dragon was right. The Roman Empire was worth his energy and sacrifice, even if he did not understand why. It was his duty to get married and to defend the Empire that he wanted to pass on to his children. And if that meant offering a sacrifice to the dragon, that is what he had to do.

Still, he could not think enthusiastically about such a sacrifice. Each time he tried to make plans for bringing sheep to the dragon, he began to long for some wine and his bed. Once, he managed to write out some vague instructions for Pasikrates, but set the note aside when he thought again about the flames from the dragon's attack.

Tomorrow, he thought. I will do my duty tomorrow.

He had more wine than usual with his evening meal, so he became drowsy quickly when he tried to read in his bedroom. The sun had not yet set, so he thought about going to the courtyard to pick up more debris. The comfort of his bed and the promise of temporary oblivion, however, proved to be more enticing. He was asleep before dark.

* * *

When he awoke the next morning, Marcellus still felt lethargic. He also had a headache.

Somehow, he thought, I must manage to plan a sacrifice to the dragon today.

But it took a lot of energy to even meet with Pasikrates after breakfast. By the middle of the meeting, he was again nodding in assent to all of Pasikrates' suggestions without clearly listening to any of them. It did not help when Pasikrates told him that his father had not improved overnight. Nor did it help that the situation on the estate reminded him of the dragon, which in turn reminded him of the sacrifice he promised. Remembering his promise made it clear that he did not seem to have the energy to do that or much of anything else.

Pasikrates continued talking. "Most of the courtyard has been cleared, thanks in part to your help, master, and no one has reported any damage to the crops. We thought that the beast ate four sheep, but we found two in a thicket on the edge of the fields. We also found a slave dead nearby. He was old and sick, so he probably died before the beast attacked. Oh! I almost forgot. Agathon is –"

He stopped speaking, looking past Marcellus toward the doorway. Marcellus turned around. Behind two slaves stood Regina. Marcellus and Pasikrates instinctively rose. The slaves and Regina moved forward. When they got close to Marcellus and Pasikrates, they moved aside while Regina, with imperious, commanding eyes, looked at Marcellus and said, loudly, "We must talk alone."

Without hesitation, Regina's slaves and Marcellus' slaves, including Pasikrates, left the room.

Marcellus felt energized as he gazed at Regina. The confidence in her posture and in her eyes reminded him of why he liked her. This feeling grew when, after the slaves left, Regina trembled slightly. She has strong emotions, Marcellus thought, and she knows when to show them and when to hide them.

"I must know, Marcellus," she said in a clear but slightly quivering voice, "I must know if it is true."

"If what is true, my dear Regina?"

Her eyes flashed briefly, as if she were angry. Still, she controlled her voice. "Did you fight with the dragon?"

Marcellus paused. "Yes."

Regina's head dropped, and she began weeping. She swayed as if she was going to collapse, so Marcellus grabbed some cushions and gently helped her down onto them. While she was still sobbing, he grabbed two more cushions and sat next to her, holding her hand. She did not resist him and continued weeping with her head down.

"My dear Marcellus," she managed to say, "I almost did not believe the dragon when he told me. Since then, I have not dared to dwell on it. Why, Marcellus? What could make you do that? You know how I feel about the dragon."

Marcellus paused again. "Perhaps, Regina, you would like some wine?"

Regina looked up with a momentary fierce expression, silently accusing Marcellus of avoiding the question. But as she looked at him, her face softened and she nodded. Marcellus filled two goblets and drank with her in silence. After a few sips and deep breaths, Regina was able to look at Marcellus and say, "Thank you."

Marcellus knew that he had to answer her. "When I first encountered the dragon," he started. He went on to tell her of the dragon's words, his original plans, his encounter with the Christians at the old shed, and his conversation with Agathon. He talked about his uncertainty about the dragon and of his anger at the dragon's attack. Regina's face darkened when he talked about Christians and softened when he talked about himself. He noticed that she was often tempted to speak, but controlled herself so that he could finish.

When he told her about the dragon's second request for a sacrifice, she laid her head on his shoulder and let out two short sobs. She took a deep breath as she lifted her head and wiped her eyes. She looked at Marcellus with a tearful smile and touched his cheek. "My dear Marcellus. I have heard about your dear father, too."

Marcellus hung his head. Before anger welled up in him, Regina stroked his shoulder. "My dear Marcellus, if only you had sacrificed those two sheep. Your father would be well right now. We could even be drinking wine with him."

Marcellus looked up. Regina was now smiling with no trace of tears. Then suddenly, her eyes were filled with the desperate longing he had seen at her estate. She spoke in a semi-whispered, rushed voice. "Even now, even now, my dear Marcellus, the dragon will accept your sacrifice. I will see to it! The dragon is indeed merciful. When I intercede for you, he will accept your sacrifice, I know it! I have already interceded for you once: when my father found out about your attack on the dragon, he was ready to cancel the wedding. 'What about the Empire?' he said. 'What about your children? Do you want them in league with Christians, along with your husband?' I calmed him down, but only by promising to come and hear the truth from you. Now I have heard it, and I know you will sacrifice now! I know you will!"

Her eyes pleaded earnestly. Their ardor was exactly what Marcellus needed to begin making arrangements for such a sacrifice.

"I will, Regina. I will bring the sacrifice tomorrow."

Regina fell into his arms, embracing him. In between sobs and breaths, she whispered, "For our children, and their children, and their children."

Regina collected herself and wiped her eyes again. She smiled at Marcellus. "And the dragon must eat, of course. And who will feed him if not us?"

Marcellus smiled at this odd thought, and Regina laughed at herself too. "It is true, though, my dear Marcellus. Would the stomach ever get food if the hands did not grab anything?"

Marcellus smiled again. "Of course not, my dear Regina."

Regina's softened eyes caught his, and she rested her head on his shoulder. Again, she gave herself over to soft tears.

CHAPTER THIRTEEN

A CHRISTIAN FUNERAL

The next morning, as the sun became visible above the trees, Marcellus and Kopto plodded on flat, untilled land with three sheep. Marcellus had left his room as the sun appeared over the horizon, collected the sheep without the help of any slaves, and slowly trudged past crops and through pastures to the edge of the estate.

Marcellus' unthinking, methodical footsteps reflected his mood. Although he desired to please Regina, he was not eager to see the dragon again. For Regina's sake, he again tried to conjure the awe and desire to surrender he felt when he first looked at the dragon's eyes. But thoughts of the blackened buildings and his father's frozen gaze always interfered and even threatened to rekindle his wrath toward the creature. He motivated himself with thoughts of the Empire, Regina, and his future children.

"I will not be disloyal," he said to himself as the sheep plodded on.

His battle experience helped. After retreats and even after victories, days of resignation and numbness often came. He learned quickly during those times that he still had to give orders, plan ahead, watch for the enemy, manage unruly soldiers, and communicate with his superiors. Without a commitment to the Empire that surpassed his emotions, he knew, he would have been an easy target for an enemy on many occasions. He had, indeed, taken advantage of numbed and disordered enemies at such times. Certain Sassanid tribes, he had learned, were particularly vulnerable when their leaders had to retreat. These leaders could keep order for a short while, but with even the slightest bit of honor gone, they lost the desire to fight after a day or two.

So he simply went on with Kopto and the three sheep, despite the heaviness in his mind.

He did not even think of Agathon until he heard singing again. With a slight breeze blowing, the voices were faint and indistinct. Marcellus noticed that they came from over a small, barren ridge that was still within the estate, so he detoured Kopto and the sheep toward them. As he came over the ridge, he immediately recognized Agathon and many of the people who had been in the old shed. Agathon was again wearing a robe, and the others were gathered around him. Behind Agathon was a wide, freshly dug hole, and outside the hole was a shroud-wrapped body.

As Marcellus moved closer, he noticed that many of the people were weeping while they were singing. One woman was closely surrounded by others, as if they were keeping her from falling. As he moved even closer, he recognized the woman as the wife of the slave who had died during the dragon attack.

The singing stopped. Agathon turned around and began chanting something. He stopped suddenly when he saw Marcellus, and the others turned and murmured as they recognized him. Agathon quickly began chanting again, and everyone turned back toward him.

Marcellus quickly realized that Agathon was chanting a story from memory. The breeze rose and fell, so he could not hear all of it, but he gathered that it was a story about Jesus visiting a friend and then raising someone from the dead.

Marcellus was not surprised by the story. He had heard and read similar legends about miraculous deeds from many other sources. A few details caught his attention, though. The friend of Jesus was

"Behind Agathon was a wide, freshly dug hole, and outside the hole was a shroud-wrapped body."

a woman, and Jesus seemed to talk with her just as he talked with the men around him. Also, the story was simple – almost absurdly simple, Marcellus thought. There were no earthquakes or lightning bolts accompanying the miracle, and no Zeus, Apollo, or Athena guiding the action while disguised as a human. There was just Jesus, a request made by a friend, a short prayer, and then a miracle. The simplicity, Marcellus thought, made the story more powerful.

Marcellus was surprised by what Agathon did next. He did not resume chanting or praying after the story. Instead, he began speaking. His voice was loud, clear, and bold, so much so that Marcellus could hear it through an upturn in the breeze. Marcellus moved himself, Kopto, and the sheep closer to the gathering.

"My dear brothers and sisters," began Agathon as he slowly looked at all the people around him, "let us think about what happens when a man dies. Perhaps you have heard legends about the happy hunting grounds or the isles of the blessed where great heroes go to live out eternity in bliss and ease. Perhaps you have heard and been frightened by the unhappy picture of the underworld in Virgil and Homer, where all men and women – nobles like Achilles and Agamemnon and the treacherous like Clytamnestra – exist in bodiless grayness and despair. Perhaps you have heard the Platonists speak of a righteous judgment of a soul after death, with wicked souls sent to torment while righteous souls are sent to live with the gods. Our Lord Jesus speaks of a heaven and a hell, but he does not clearly answer that simple question: What happens to a man when he dies? And most especially, what is happening to the soul of Synderikos, who lies before us?

"The answer comes from Our Lord through the Apostle Paul. It is not an answer that any Platonist or legend will give. It offers no comfort that way, nor does it promise the comfort offered by soothsayers and magicians who claim to contact the souls of the dead. Many would say that it is not a direct answer at all, and they are right. But it is full of comfort for those who mourn. The answer from the Apostle Paul is this: Christians who die are asleep in the Lord.

"What wisdom is contained in these simple words! With the word 'asleep,' the Apostle Paul reminds us that death is not the end for a man or a woman. He reminds us that we were made to live forever with our God. With the words 'in the Lord,' he does away with the question itself. The Apostle Paul does not offer legends or hopeful stories to dispel the fear, anguish, or grief of one who asks, 'What happens to a man when he dies?' He says that the Christian who dies is 'in the Lord.' In the Lord, who himself died and defeated death. In the Lord, who gave us baptism so that we could die and be raised with him. In the Lord, whose triumph over death makes the Apostle Paul say that nothing – not rulers, not masters, not angels, not demons, not sin, not death – can separate us from the love of God. That is our comfort. The servant of God Synderikos, who was baptized, who lived humbly before God with us, who was a forgiven sinner, who was killed by a beast spawned from the evil one, is with the Lord, the Lord of life. On the last day, he will be raised to live eternally on the glorious new earth that the Lord even now prepares for us.

"Let us mourn, then, and let us weep. Death is real and bitter. Let us also accept the Apostle Paul's word of comfort. Synderikos is asleep in the Lord, who is alive and glorified in the heavens and on the earth. In the name of the Father and of the Son and of the Holy Spirit, Amen!"

The people in the crowd shouted, "Amen!" They embraced each other with smiles and tears on their faces. Even Agathon wept before he turned around and chanted again.

Marcellus felt as if he had been awakened or as if a cloud had been lifted from his eyes. Agathon's words shocked him. Marcellus automatically thought of Diocletian and Julius Caesar when he heard the word "Lord," yet for Agathon and all the people around the grave, Jesus was the Lord. They believed that this Jesus, this Jewish peasant, was alive and ruling the world. It was so absurd, yet something in Marcellus wanted to believe it.

And Agathon had spoken about Synderikos not as a slave, but as this Lord's servant. Marcellus' ownership of this man was absolutely irrelevant to Agathon and the other Christians. As he looked at the gathering in front of him, he again saw a shocking mixture of free men and slaves, men and women, rich and poor.

Marcellus was also amazed that this slave's funeral would be like a funeral for a nobleman like his father or some high-ranking army officer. Even when he had had time, he had not buried fellow officers in the army with such attention. In fact, he usually followed the army's maxim, "bury and forget." These Christians, Marcellus could not help but notice, did not want to "bury and forget." They wanted to remember this slave. Furthermore, they were able to see a corpse without fear for themselves. They grieved openly, yet they also believed, somehow, that the slave had won some kind of victory over death.

This idea – that one could defeat death – struck Marcellus as absurd. Yet again, he could not help wanting to believe it, to join these people in their prayers and tears. He wanted to say "Amen!" to the bold words of Agathon.

Agathon stopped chanting, and the funeral party started breaking up. Two people – Marcellus recognized them as slaves from his estate – were hurriedly burying the corpse, while the others started walking up the small ridge past Marcellus. Marcellus looked for Pasikrates, but could not find him. As he looked, he noticed several small mounds like the one being created over the corpse.

This is where the dead slaves are, Marcellus thought. This is why the slave ditch is empty.

Agathon walked to Marcellus and bowed. "Hello, Marcellus. I did not expect to see you today."

Marcellus decided to be abrupt. "You are the one burying the slaves from my father's estate," he said.

Surprised, Agathon only replied, "Yes, I and the other Christians. Your father gave us permission."

As Marcellus looked out on all the mounds, he counted at least twenty. "Surely these were not all Christian slaves."

"No. But we bury every slave – with your father's permission. Some even asked us to bury them, knowing that the ditch was the alternative."

Marcellus shook his head. "What I am wondering about is why you do it at all. They are slaves, after all."

Agathon's blue eyes gazed at Marcellus. "Do you mean that you will throw Pasikrates in a ditch when he dies?"

Marcellus took in a deep breath. He had never thought about Pasikrates dying. He immediately knew, though, that Agathon was right. "No, but Pasikrates is..."

"Is what?"

Marcellus' mind raced. What was special about Pasikrates? "He is my hardest working slave," he offered feebly.

"But he is just a slave," Agathon challenged.

Marcellus could think of nothing to say. Agathon challenged him again. "Pasikrates is your friend. That is why you would bury him."

Marcellus nodded. He could think of no one who had earned his deep trust like Pasikrates had. Without Pasikrates, he thought, I would worry constantly about my father and the estate. And father must have felt the same way when I was a child.

"This slave, Synderikos," said Agathon, "was someone's friend as well. He served your father loyally, along with all the other people you saw here today, especially his fellow slaves. He served his wife faithfully. He did not limit himself to helping Christians. I believe – actually, it is something all Christians should believe – that he was God's friend. You are surprised? Jesus himself said it. I have another surprise for you. This slave prayed to God for your father. All the Christians on the estate pray for your father, especially now."

Marcellus looked down, feeling a sense of shame. He knew that most of the slaves on the estate were loyal to his father, but he had not expected such love. "But why?" was all he could say.

"Why not? Jesus told us to love everyone, even our enemies. Who can say how important someone like Synderikos was? We must not ask such questions about our fellow human beings. That is why we buried him. That is why the slave ditch is empty."

Marcellus continued to look down. He could not imagine Regina speaking in such a way – or Lucius, or Demetrios, or even his father. He realized, again with shame, that he could not imagine himself saying such words, even though at this moment he wanted to. And he wanted others to speak about him and his life in a similar way.

Agathon interrupted Marcellus' thoughts. "You are going to the dragon now?"

Marcellus looked up again into Agathon's eyes and could not help but feel another wave of shame. But he saw compassion as well, and that gave him the strength to answer. "Yes."

"Would you rather join us?"

Yes, thought Marcellus. Yes. Yes.

But he thought again about Regina, Demetrios, the soldiers under his command, his father's hopes, and the hopes he had for himself. For a moment, he wondered if he could become a Christian, marry Regina, and continue to serve in the Roman Army. After all, that was what many of his soldiers did.

Just as quickly, he realized that this could never happen for him. Regina had made it clear: he had to submit to the dragon if he wanted to marry her. Marcellus also recalled Demetrios' words about the drive to eliminate Christians from the army, starting with officers like him. Marcellus knew that he was being pulled in opposite directions by two irresistible forces.

"I wish I could talk with my father," he said softly, more to himself than to Agathon.

Agathon nodded silently.

Marcellus looked up into the sky. In a loud, frustrated voice, he said, "What should I do?"

Agathon paused before answering. "You know what I would do, Marcellus. You know what I think of death – and life."

Marcellus pictured Pasikrates and the other slaves in the old shed. He did not understand it, but he knew that the path of his life needed to be with them and Agathon. He also knew that this path would most likely to lead to his death. He made a decision.

Marcellus noticed that the two slaves had finished burying Synderikos. He called them over to himself. "Walk these three sheep back to the estate," he ordered. "I must get back quickly and prepare for another dragon attack."

CHAPTER FOURTEEN

A LONG NIGHT

As the sun got closer to the horizon and began to turn orange, Marcellus sat next to some books, looking for the dragon. He felt sure that the dragon would wait until the sun was completely down to attack, but his soldier's instincts made him cautious. A clever enemy, he knew, would strike when least expected.

While looking, he continued to review all that had been done that day. Pasikrates had agreed to run the estate as normal and assign everyone to either a fire team or a military team. Throughout the day, the fire teams gathered and repaired every available bucket and put them in places that would make it easy to set up a chain from the villa's well or the fountain. The military teams were made up of slaves who used to be soldiers, most of them captives from one of Marcellus' raids or battles. Marcellus knew that it would be risky to give weapons to slaves, but most of the slaves were Christians who relished the thought of a battle over the dull work with crops and animals. These teams gathered with Marcellus, practiced throwing spears, and listened as he explained his strategy.

Marcellus knew that only a lucky shot would hurt the dragon, so his goal was to disrupt any attack and limit damage to the villa. It was a standard strategy against an enemy that was stronger: minimize losses and buy time while a new strategy was developed or reinforcements could arrive.

Marcellus sat alone while the teams organized themselves quickly and responded to his orders. Everyone, it seemed, was eager to prevent or disrupt another attack. A few slaves grumbled, saying something about giving the dragon what it wanted, but they were ignored by Marcellus, Pasikrates, and the rest of the people on the estate.

While he sat and watched for the dragon, he reflected on the reading he had done that afternoon. Agathon had handed him a small book, saying, "If you will join us, you should start reading." It was, according to Agathon, the Gospel of Matthew, a biography of Jesus. Pleased with the good condition of the book, Marcellus read it eagerly and quickly.

Much of it puzzled him. It began with a meaningless genealogy and was peppered with barely believable events like a meeting with some sort of demon in the desert and angels appearing to Jesus' mother. These were, thought Marcellus, clumsy attempts to divinize Jesus. He also found the story of the virgin birth fantastical, but at least he appreciated its irony. Similar stories were told about many emperors, backing their claim to be "Lord" and "sons of the gods." Now, the story was being told about a Jewish peasant from a land far away from Rome. Whoever Matthew was, thought Marcellus, he knew how to get the attention of a Roman reader like himself.

As Marcellus followed the story of Jesus' ministry, he was surprised to discover that now Jesus no longer seemed to be naïve and simple. This man obviously had some sort of power – some of the healing stories, he thought, must have been true – and he was a natural leader. Yet he used his power and his leadership in unusual ways, and he spent most of his time with the wrong people: the poor, tax collectors, the sick and dying. He was not generous as Cicero conceived generosity, where people who are noble and wealthy bestow gifts on the lesser-born and poorer friends. Jesus really seemed to love these lowly people, even to prefer their company. Marcellus began to see why the slaves on his estate along with noble men like Agathon would be attracted to Jesus.

Reading the story of Jesus reminded Marcellus of his mother, one of the few Christians he had known as a young boy. He did not remember much: her hair, her smile, a scowl at one of his childish misdeeds, a story told to him and some other children. He had never thought about her much, for he had no siblings and the subject obviously caused pain for his father. He remembered the only words his father had said about her. She was, according to him, dutiful, obedient, diligent, a good manager of the estate, and someone who loved her husband and child.

Marcellus looked back at the book and realized that it was now too dark to read. The sky's orange, purple, and dark blue told him that it was time to make one last tour of the villa before darkness was complete. He doubted if he could concentrate or read much more anyway. He had to assume the role of a military commander. He knew that everyone on the villa, like his soldiers, was watching him, so he had to show that he was in command of the situation. But he naturally felt like he had to be active, to make sure, once again, that all the buckets, spears, and people were in their proper places with their instructions.

* * *

As much as he could, Marcellus appreciated the bright, clear stars for their beauty and the light breeze that helped him stay awake. He was still keeping watch for the dragon, as were others on the estate. As darkness had descended and the stars slowly appeared, he had received reports from around the estate, moved to different locations in the villa, and encouraged others as their attentiveness flagged. Marcellus knew that the onset of sleepiness made it a perfect time to attack, and he knew that the dragon was cunning enough to think of it.

A crash and several loud shouts pierced the silence. Marcellus sprang across the courtyard toward the voices that continued to yell. He saw three or four torches assemble near the edge of the villa.

The voices softened by the time he arrived. He saw two slaves on the ground, surrounded by a small crowd. The ground around them was littered with buckets.

Pasikrates was the first one to notice Marcellus. "Master! Nothing to worry about here, nothing at all! Just some bungling slaves."

The people around Pasikrates laughed at this remark, and Pasikrates himself smiled sheepishly.

Eventually, the story became clear. One slave, perched on a ledge and supposedly looking for the dragon, had dozed off and crashed into another sleeping slave on the ground. Their shouts had brought other slaves running. Pasikrates had arrived first, but without a torch in hand, he had run into a stack of buckets and sent them scattering loudly. This caused more shouts, more slaves racing to the scene, and more crashing buckets.

Marcellus smiled when the last details of the story were told. "Let us quickly stack these buckets and return to our places. An attack may still come in the darkness that is left." He paused, then added, "And Pasikrates – no more bungling."

Another round of laughter erupted, and Pasikrates joined in. Marcellus moved back to his place to look for a moving dark patch against the stars, but he saw nothing unusual.

The sky grew brighter before the sun broke the horizon, but Marcellus was still tense. He could feel the nervous mood in the villa slowly transform into one of relaxed and subdued jubilance. This would be a good time to attack, he thought, but he did not bother to waken those who had fallen asleep.

By the time the sun was in full view, all the people of the estate were gathered at the fountain, informally celebrating. Many were splashing themselves and each other in mock efforts to stay awake. On Marcellus' orders, Pasikrates handed out bread and cheese to everyone, and that made the mood even more celebratory.

"Look! Callis is coming!"

Everyone turned and watched a figure half-run, half-stumble in from a field. As he got closer, Marcellus could see that he was carrying something. He stumbled into the villa and fell down near Marcellus' feet, panting. Several slaves moved to get him some water. In his right hand, he held up a small parchment. Draped over his left shoulder, with pieces of doughy flesh dangling haphazardly off of it, was a portion of a bloodied sheepskin.

CHAPTER FIFTEEN

A THIRD MEETING
WITH REGINA

After Callis handed the parchment to Marcellus and guzzled some water, Pasikrates broke the silence. "What does it say?"

Marcellus quickly read the parchment. He did not want to answer. But when he saw that all eyes were focused on him, he knew that he had to. They are like soldiers, he thought. They need the truth in order to keep trusting me.

"It is from Cephalus, the commander of the nearby army post," he announced loudly. It says, 'To the tribune Marcellus, greetings. Twelve of your sheep are missing. I have taken them at the request of the dragon.'"

A murmur of dismay ran through the people at the fountain.

Like me, Marcellus thought angrily to himself, they feel tricked. While protecting the villa, he – and they – had left the fields and pastures open to a raid. Moreover, they now realized that they had two enemies that they could not fight: the dragon and the local soldiers of the Roman army. And then there was the horrible sense that this was certainly not the last raid.

Marcellus thought quickly, then spoke in a commanding tone. "Today, we rest as much as possible. Only the bare minimum of work should be done. I think we are safe during the day, but the dragon may attack again tonight, and we have to be ready. Pasikrates and I will find a new way to protect the estate in the days to come."

As the people drifted off to their beds or their duties, a rider approached the villa from another field. When it was close enough, Marcellus recognized it as one of Lucius' slaves. The slave dismounted in front of Marcellus, bowed, and handed Pasikrates a small piece of parchment.

"The lady Regina requests that the tribune Marcellus visit her immediately at her father's villa."

Marcellus simply shook his head when Pasikrates offered him the parchment. "You are in charge," he sighed. "Hopefully, I will be back before supper."

* * *

When he arrived at Lucius' villa, Marcellus noticed that it was not busy. The slaves and guests that were there eyed him coldly. When Marcellus was told that Lucius was busy and could not greet him, he knew that Lucius was intentionally snubbing him.

After being forced to wait, standing, Marcellus was led to a room where he was told Regina would meet him. Again, there was no place to sit down, and again, he waited for a long time before Regina and two slaves entered the room. Regina greeted Marcellus stiffly and formally, and Marcellus returned the formality. He was not offered any water or wine.

When Regina dismissed the slaves, her bearing changed. She tried to stay formal, but before she could say anything, she began weeping quietly. Marcellus said nothing.

"Why have you not sacrificed to the dragon?" Regina finally managed to ask.

Marcellus knew that such a question was coming. "I am sorry, my dear Regina, but I do not have an answer that will satisfy you."

Regina quickly looked up at him with stern, dark eyes. For a moment, the expression in them reminded Marcellus of the dragon's seemingly bottomless, consuming eyes. Something else quickly came over her, though, and she looked down and started weeping again.

"Please, Marcellus, please," she said in a broken voice. "I would be a good wife and mother – I want nothing more. Like you, I love the Empire. Think of our fathers, dear Marcellus. Think of the hopes that will go unfulfilled if we do not marry. Think of the children that will not be born, the sons who will be future soldiers like you and your father and his father. Please, please."

Briefly, Marcellus was tempted again to think that he could have all of these things. Despite his tiredness, however, he remembered the parchment from Cephalus, the bloodied hide on Callis, the burned buildings, the now-repellant dragon's eyes, and his lifeless father. He breathed in deeply. "I am sorry, Regina, but I cannot do it."

Regina immediately looked up angrily and moved closer to Marcellus. "You are a dishonest, disloyal man! How could you have become a tribune in the army? How could anyone have trusted you with anything? My father has connections to Galerius. He will make sure you never rise more in the army! And you deserve such a fate!"

She stared at Marcellus with fiery eyes, breathing hard. He did not say anything, but he knew that his undropped gaze continued to say, "I cannot do it." Suddenly, Regina ran to Marcellus, knelt down in front of him, and began weeping again.

"Forgive me, my dear Marcellus, forgive me. I know how good and noble you are. I know that you are a good soldier for the Empire." She looked up at him. "Please, please, it is not too late. I spoke with the dragon yesterday. I brought a slave to the dragon, a sick old woman. You can do the same, and the dragon will accept it! He will call you his friend! Your estate is bigger than ours, so you must be able to find someone who will die soon anyway." Her eyes brightened. "A Christian! Even an old and sick one. Someone who will die anyway – that would please the dragon more than anything. Will you, my dear Marcellus? Please." Her eyes drooped with tears.

Marcellus thought of Synderikos and the funeral fit for a nobleman. He silently took off his armband and set it on the floor next to Regina.

As he walked out of the room, Marcellus heard Regina let out a desperate, despairing sob.

CHAPTER SIXTEEN

ANOTHER DREAM

When Marcellus returned to his estate, he immediately put himself to work. He wanted to make sure everything was in place for another attack, and he knew that work was the best remedy for the fatigue that kept washing over him. He had nearly fallen off Kopto twice on the ride home from Lucius' estate. If Kopto had not been so familiar with his riding style, he could easily have been left in a barren field until the next day.

Reviewing the supplies and plans did not take long, mostly because Pasikrates had somehow managed to do most of the work before he returned. Pasikrates also informed him that all of the animals were accounted for except the twelve sheep that Cephalus had taken.

Suddenly, Marcellus realized his mistake. He looked at the sky. There is still time, he thought. He cursed himself and, fighting another wave of tiredness, he barked at Pasikrates, "Send slaves to get the animals to the villa!"

Pasikrates, looking tired and surprised, said, "Why, master?"

"Do it, you fool! Did we not learn last night that the animals are not safe in the fields? And arrange for some food in my room immediately."

Pasikrates nodded, not seeming to notice Marcellus' sharp tone. Marcellus turned his back and marched quickly to his room.

* * *

"Can I help in any way, Marcellus?"

Marcellus looked up and saw Agathon in his doorway. He motioned for Agathon to enter.

The food he was hoping for had not yet arrived, and the waves of tiredness were coming more frequently. He could not help replying to Agathon in a harsh tone: "It would be a dishonor to have a guest work for me. I am surprised that you would suggest it."

"I am afraid I have offended you again. Forgive me."

Marcellus waved his hand in acceptance. He ran his hand through his hair and sighed. As he closed his eyes, he started to lose the desire to open them again. Maybe I can sleep while talking with Agathon, he thought. Pictures of his last conversation with Agathon drifted into his mind.

Something hard hit his head. He tried to turn around to see what had hit him, but found himself rolling on the floor. Then he was pulled up to a sitting position, looking at Agathon.

"You're exhausted," said Agathon. Agathon turned his head and said, "Bring some water over here, quickly! And grab some pillows!"

Marcellus looked over Agathon's shoulder and saw a slave holding a tray with two pitchers and some food. He closed his eyes and would have drifted off again if Agathon had not pressed a cup to his lips.

"Some water," said Agathon. "Then some food and wine. When was the last time you ate?"

Marcellus struggled to think while he swallowed. "Last night, maybe yesterday afternoon." He shook his head, trying to revive himself. He drank some more water and looked up at Agathon. "Thank you," he said softly. Feeling stronger, he added, with a small smile, "Please join me for some food."

Agathon laughed and held Marcellus as the slave put pillows around them. Agathon was about to lower Marcellus on to the pillows, but Marcellus said, "I can do it. You can let go."

"Are you sure?"

"Let me try."

Agathon released his grip on Marcellus, and Marcellus was able to remain sitting upright. He lowered himself on to some pillows and grabbed some fruit from the platter in front of him. He ate quickly, knowing that it would revive him further. When he noticed that Agathon was not eating, he said, "You must eat, Agathon. It is rude of me to eat in front of a guest."

Agathon nodded, picked up some olives, and began eating them.

Agathon broke the silence after he and Marcellus had nearly finished the food and wine. "I notice that your armband is gone," he said, looking at Marcellus.

Marcellus was feeling strong enough to sit up. He drank another goblet of water, wondering how much he should tell Agathon. Even though he felt clear-headed, he knew that another spell of tiredness could come at any time, so he did not trust his own judgment.

"I broke my engagement with Regina," was all he said.

Agathon nodded, seemingly picking up on Marcellus' reluctance to speak.

"At the risk of offending you again, I offer you my help," said Agathon. He pointed out the window. "There is still some time before the sun goes down. Why not sleep a little? Either I or Pasikrates can wake you if the dragon comes."

Marcellus resisted this thought at first, but then nodded. The food and wine had given him a clearer head, and he realized that he would be better prepared for an attack if he slept. He also heard what Agathon had not said directly: If the dragon came at all, it probably would not come until nightfall.

"A quick bath, then sleep," Marcellus agreed. "I thank you for your offer and expect to repay you."

"If you continue to let me visit the Christians here, I will consider that payment enough."

Marcellus nodded again. It was, he realized, a fair arrangement, and it made him feel that he was not dishonoring himself by accepting Agathon's help. He ate another piece of cheese and finished his goblet of wine. Feeling even stronger, he stood up and was pleased that it was not difficult to do so. Agathon rose with him.

"To the baths, then," he said as he smiled and bowed to Agathon.

* * *

The bath made Marcellus ready to sleep even before he returned to his room. He tried to review the plans he had made with Pasikrates, but only recalled the location of the animals before falling asleep.

When he opened his eyes, he was looking at an island. He looked down and saw that he was, somehow, standing on top of the water, with waves regularly rolling over his feet and calves. Something is familiar about this, he thought. He stood there, puzzling, and decided to look around. Behind him, not far away, was a boat traveling toward him and the island.

When he heard the singing, he understood. The singing was coming from the boat, and he knew that he was standing between it and the island that was breaking up. When he turned around to look again at the island, his thought was confirmed. He saw two fissures branching throughout the island.

"Marcellus!"

The voice came from the boat. When Marcellus turned around again, he was surprised to see Agathon in front of the boat, waving to him. He waved back and was happy that Agathon somehow started to pilot the boat directly toward him.

Although he heard a rumble behind him, he did not take his eyes off the boat. As it got closer, Marcellus peered more closely at Agathon. But he had seemingly changed, becoming shorter with brown eyes, darker skin and longer hair. The man's eyes remained locked on Marcellus, and the boat kept moving in Marcellus' direction.

By the time Marcellus could touch the boat, he knew that the man was not Agathon. He felt like he recognized the man, but also knew that he had never seen him before. The man's brown eyes gazed steadily at Marcellus. The man held out his hand.

"Will you come aboard?"

Marcellus felt like he could not lie to this man. "I do not know," he said.

The man smiled. "Do you have anywhere else to go?"

Marcellus looked back at the island. More fissures had appeared, and some of it seemed to have crumbled into the sea. When he looked back at the man, he asked, "How long can I remain here?"

To his surprise, the man nearly laughed out loud. It was not a demeaning laugh, and it made Marcellus realize that his question was rather silly. If it had not been for the continuing stern and compassionate gaze, he would have felt ashamed. Instead, he reached out, grabbed the man's hand, and stepped on to the boat.

Immediately, the scene changed. He was somewhere near the middle of the island. He could not see the boat, but everyone from the boat was scattering over the island. Not far away, he spied the man with the brown eyes, and somehow he knew that everyone spreading over the island was following his orders.

He watched the people with interest. Some began repairing fissures, some were able to stop fissures from spreading, and some stood together and made plans for the future. He noticed others preparing and distributing food, while others began to build roads and houses, sometimes directly over repaired fissures. Many performed mundane tasks like tilling the soil and minding children. Many returned to the man with brown eyes and received instructions before spreading back out on the island.

"Marcellus!"

The man with the brown eyes was calling. Marcellus felt like he had to go to him. When he arrived at the spot where the man stood, he realized that he was on the highest point on the island. The man kept his gaze upon Marcellus.

"The man's hand moved upward, and Marcellus saw, far above the ships, the dragon circling."

"Will you join us?" he asked.

Marcellus had known that the man was going to ask this question. He hesitated, responding to a vague uneasiness inside him.

"Do not be afraid," the man said.

When Marcellus looked back at the man's inviting eyes, he knew what the answer had to be. He did not desire to lose himself in those eyes, but felt that they gave him a new desire to live as himself – a better self, but still himself.

"Yes," Marcellus responded.

The man smiled again, and Marcellus felt a wave of pleasure pass through his body and mind. It was, it seemed, an extension of the pleasure that the man felt.

"Look, Marcellus," the man commanded. Marcellus followed the man's finger to the sea, where he saw hundreds of ships like the one the man had been on. The man's hand moved upward, and Marcellus saw, far above the ships, the dragon circling. Suddenly, the dragon dove toward the ships.

"Protect my ships," said the man.

The dragon roared, and fire came out of its mouth. It would soon be able to spit flames at the ships and their passengers. Marcellus did not know what to do.

"How? How can I protect them?"

The roar grew louder.

"Protect my ships," the man said again.

The roar grew even louder. Soon, it was deafening. Marcellus shouted in desperation.

Then, he woke up. Again, the roar continued, and again, he knew that the dragon was attacking the villa.

CHAPTER SEVENTEEN

ANOTHER ATTACK

As Marcellus sat up, Pasikrates rushed into the room. Without speaking, they each understood what had to be done. Pasikrates rushed out. He is in charge of the fire crews, thought Marcellus, and I am the soldier.

Marcellus quickly tied on his sandals and left his room. He immediately looked for the dragon against the starry sky, but saw nothing. To his relief, he could not smell or see anything burning at the villa. In the distance, along the edge of a pasture, he counted three trees burning. That whole grove might be lost, he thought.

Marcellus began to move to the closest place where weapons had been placed. Then suddenly, an ear-splitting roar came from above him, followed by shouts from people and sounds from terrified animals. Bursts of flame appeared near a rooftop. Marcellus saw an array of glittering scales leap from there to another part of the roof. He also dimly saw several people scrambling with a ladder and, he presumed, a series of buckets under the burning rooftop.

Heartened, he became determined to distract attention away from them. He moved again toward the closest battle station. Another roar followed, along with more yells and animal noises.

When the battle station was in sight, he hoped to see three men – all former soldiers from foreign armies – firing spears at the dragon. Instead, he saw them scrambling around, seemingly without purpose, and then shouting curses.

"What is happening?" he yelled as he got to them.

"Look!" one of them yelled back, pointing to the ground. There, by Marcellus' feet, lay about three dozen spears, all broken into two or more pieces.

"It was Melchior, the Persian slave," said one of the men. "He cannot be found."

Marcellus remembered a surly, unkempt man. Pasikrates, he was sure, had complained about him recently. Probably one of the dragon-worshipping thieves that father mentioned, thought Marcellus.

With controlled anger, Marcellus grabbed a spear that had been broken in half. He moved to the edge of the courtyard and looked for the dragon. With three fires now burning, it was easy to spot the mass of scales on top of a roof on the other side of the courtyard. He took two steps and threw the spear. As he expected, it fell far short of its target.

"You will have to use the longest pieces and throw when the dragon is closer," he ordered. "Tell me now: how long has it been dark?"

The three men looked at him, puzzled.

"Tell me, how long!"

"The night is not half over, master."

Marcellus shut his eyes and tried to drive away the anguish in his mind. The dragon had much more time to do damage, and Melchior would have all night to walk or run to safety at Lucius' estate. Once again, he had been tricked.

"Do we have any other weapons?" he asked.

Just then, another deafening roar came from above. Marcellus and the three other men covered their ears. The dragon landed in the middle of the courtyard, clutching a limp, headless sheep carcass in its claws. Looking around the courtyard, it hissed and seemed to grin triumphantly. All the slaves putting out fires fled the courtyard in terror.

Then, the dragon did something that surprised Marcellus. It threw the carcass a short distance, then dove on it as if it were playing with it. Then it rolled onto its back with the carcass between its front claws. It ate some of the torn animal, then rolled all the way over and ate the rest. Then, like a horse in a field, it wriggled on its back, rolled twice, and wriggled some more. The dragon was relishing its victory, and Marcellus had to fight back the wrath that told him to charge the dragon with nothing other than a broken spear.

By the time he and the other men could have thrown anything, the dragon had flown away. Marcellus ran to the other battle stations, finding all of the other spears broken as well. When the dragon returned with another sheep in its claws, he and others threw half-spears, but nothing could be aimed well enough or thrown hard enough to even cause the dragon to notice.

For the rest of the night, Marcellus helped put out fires and watched as the dragon devoured more animals.

CHAPTER EIGHTEEN

A DECISION AND A REQUEST

Marcellus sat beside his father's bed, reading. His father was still unconscious. His face was sunken and pale, and his breathing was irregular. Marcellus knew that if his father did not involuntarily swallow water every once in a while, he would have already died. Even now, Marcellus had very little hope that his father would live more than a few days.

Marcellus was reading some copies of letters written by a man the Christians called "the Apostle Paul." Agathon had given them to him. They were, he found, an antidote to the cycles of anger and despair he felt as he thought about the dragon, his father, and the estate. In these letters, Marcellus found an exuberant, almost reckless love alongside an unconquerable belief in a divine kingdom that was alive and conquering the current kingdoms of the earth. Marcellus realized that Paul, as an unimportant Jew from a remote part of the Empire, had even less reason to believe in such ideas than he himself did – and still, Paul believed, unshakably.

He was not surprised that, like the Gospel he had read earlier, these letters contained much that he did not understand. But he could not deny Paul's passion for goodness, his love for the people to whom he wrote, and his conviction that divine power had been given to human beings. This assertion, more than anything else, set Paul apart from Cicero in Marcellus' eyes. Cicero believed in goodness, to be sure, but he did not come close to Paul's belief that a god gave his own life in order to live in the hearts and minds of ordinary people, even slaves.

And that was another thing about Paul that surprised him. Paul was almost completely indifferent to emperors, governors, generals, and the like. Cicero always seemed to presume that human life would get better with the judicious exercise of political power. But for Paul, the change the world needed would come from the obscure Christian communities that received his letters.

Marcellus heard a voice behind him and turned to see Pasikrates and Agathon enter the room.

"Thank you for coming," said Marcellus, standing up.

"What do you need, Marcellus?" asked Agathon.

"I do not need anything. But I would like you to pray for my father."

"Of course. May Pasikrates join me?"

Marcellus nodded silently. Agathon and Pasikrates moved to his father, with Agathon lightly touching Titus' head and Pasikrates gently holding a hand.

Marcellus remembered reading about the miraculous healings performed by Jesus, and he had heard from Agathon that such healings still happened. He could not help but picture his father opening his eyes and returning to his life on the estate. But he did not hope for such an outcome. He had seen enough death and illness to know their force, and he knew that Christians were not foolish enough to claim to be able to end both.

After a few moments of silence, Agathon said quietly, "Heavenly Father, you healed the sick and raised the dead through your son Jesus Christ and the Holy Spirit. Visit and heal Titus that he might rise and give thanks and praise to your holy name. Amen."

"Amen," whispered Pasikrates with a sob.

After Agathon prayed, Titus' breathing slowed and deepened. Marcellus thought that his face became somewhat less pale. Other than that, he could detect no change.

"Thank you," said Marcellus to Agathon, still looking at his father.

"Do you need anything else?" asked Agathon.

Marcellus paused. "Again, I do not need anything, but I would like to ask you something."

"Of course."

Silence followed. Realizing that Agathon would not think of it, Marcellus turned and said, "Pasikrates, I would like to speak with Agathon alone."

Pasikrates looked embarrassed and said, "Yes, master, right away," and hurried out the door.

Agathon sighed. "If you want to talk about your father, Marcellus, no one knows him better than Pasikrates."

"I do not want to talk about my father. I want to talk about me."

Agathon did not say anything, but Marcellus could tell from his eyes that he was surprised. Marcellus continued, "Thank you again for your help here. You may stay at this estate as long as you wish."

"I cannot stay long – or, I should not stay long. I suspect that the dragon knows I am here, and I do not want the people on the estate to be in more danger than they already are."

"When will you go?"

"Tomorrow – or today, if you wish."

So, thought Marcellus, the time for my decision has to be now. He knew, though, that the decision was already made. He only had to act on it.

Marcellus hesitated. He was no longer troubled by thoughts of Regina, and he knew that army life was over for him. He also knew that he could only stay on the estate if he submitted to the dragon, and he would not do that. And whatever lies the dragon had told, Marcellus believed it when it said that it had lived – and would probably continue to live – for a long time. Even if the dragon were dead, he reasoned, Cephalus would probably continue to harass or even plunder the estate.

Marcellus had conceded to himself that the situation was hopeless. Yet he had felt calm as he came to that conclusion at his father's bedside, reading the Apostle Paul's letters. Still, it was hard to act on his decision to become a Christian. He knew that as a Christian, he would not gain any ability to protect his estate and his slaves. He would not be able to stop Galerius' persecution of Christians. And he would become an outlaw in the Empire that he loved. Words of Jesus came to his mind: "But seek first the kingdom of God and his righteousness, and all these things will be given you besides. Do not worry about tomorrow; tomorrow will take care of itself. Sufficient for a day is its own evil." At first, these words had sounded soothing, but now he realized that they also demanded a deep sacrifice. They were, Marcellus concluded, like the stern and inviting brown eyes of the man in his dream.

Marcellus took a deep breath. First, he would ask Agathon the most pressing question. "What do you think I should do?"

Agathon surprised Marcellus with the quickness of his reply. "I have thought about your situation, Marcellus. I have prayed, too. I am sorry, but I can think of no solution to your troubles."

Marcellus paused, then leaped in his mind. "What if I became a Christian?"

Agathon surprised Marcellus again, this time with laughter. "You will only get new troubles."

Marcellus smiled weakly and nodded. I will have to leap again, he thought. "I would like to be baptized," he said softly, not looking at Agathon.

Agathon almost said something, then waited for Marcellus' eyes to meet his own. Then he smiled. "We will start preparing tomorrow. You can be baptized at the end of the year."

"No," answered Marcellus, "baptize me tomorrow."

Agathon's eyes grew wide. Marcellus knew he had to explain himself. "I know it is unusual, but think of my situation again. The dragon will not rest until I am dead and the Christians of this estate are dead or scattered. What about Pasikrates and the others? I want to fight this dragon, but I know very well that my life will be in more danger than ever if I do. That is why I should be baptized tomorrow."

"I understand, but it is very unusual. I am not sure."

"I did not think you would be. Let me tell you about a dream I had right before the dragon attacked again."

Marcellus related the dream with the man, the island, the ships, and the dragon. When he finished, he said, "That is why I think it is my time to act. And I do not want to act without being baptized."

Agathon closed his eyes. For what seemed like a long time, he did not open them. Marcellus waited.

"You realize," Agathon said without opening his eyes, "that what I said before was true. Baptism will not solve your problems or protect you from this dragon."

"I understand."

Agathon remained silent for another long period. Then, he opened his eyes and simply said, "Very well. Tomorrow." He got up and bowed. "I must prepare, and you must devote your hours to prayer. I will return soon and we will discuss this more." He bowed again and walked out the door.

Marcellus closed his eyes. He felt as if he were trembling. "Lord, have mercy on me as I prepare to be baptized tomorrow," he whispered.

CHAPTER NINETEEN

THE BAPTISM

The next day, Marcellus stood near the courtyard fountain, wrapped in a rough blanket. Agathon chanted prayers while the other Christians from the estate occasionally sang responses. Pasikrates stood next to him with silent tears running down his cheeks. Agathon had told him that he needed a sponsor, and Marcellus had chosen Pasikrates.

To Marcellus' surprise, some of the Christians from neighboring estates had come to his baptism. The only way they could be there, he figured, was if one or more of the slaves from his father's estate had given up yet more sleep to bring the announcement.

Marcellus did his best to listen to all of the prayers. Many times, Agathon chanted something that he did not understand or recognize. When he did hear something familiar, he would focus on it and think about it, and in the process miss the prayer that followed. He did not get frustrated, however. Agathon had explained to him that baptism was God was killing him, raising him up, and bringing him into the body of Christ. If Marcellus had had more time, he would have had to memorize all the baptismal prayers. "But follow the service as best as you can and enjoy it," were Agathon's last words of advice.

Marcellus was enjoying it, especially the faces of the people gathered around him. Most of them he knew as slaves, but now, he knew, they would become brothers and sisters – and, to his surprise, he felt that way too. More than once, while looking at those singing, he mumbled, "Thank you, Lord." He tried not to look at Pasikrates' face, for it made him want to weep as well.

Marcellus' mind kept coming back to the new name he would receive at his baptism. Agathon had told him that the name was usually taken from a martyr, a hero of the church, or some person in the Christian writings. Sometimes, the name signified something important about the person being baptized. Before Marcellus could think about requesting a name, Agathon had said that it was the bishop's job to choose one. He then discovered that Pasikrates was actually Mercurius and that Agathon had been Lysander.

"Now it is time for Marcellus' confession," announced Agathon. He looked at Marcellus and nodded.

Marcellus breathed deeply. "I have worshipped false gods, I have lied, I have killed men unnecessarily, I have taken what has not belonged to me, I have coveted the property and honor of others, I have not loved my God or my neighbor as I should have."

Marcellus spoke these words confidently, but they brought back the uneasy feeling in his stomach from an earlier, private confession with Agathon. By answering questions posed by Agathon, he had detailed several episodes from his life that troubled him. Some troubled him because they were clear violations of his own moral code, as when he had lied to his father about a raid that had not gone well, or when he had betrayed a fellow officer's trust in order to secure praise from Demetrios. Other episodes troubled him more deeply, for they revealed how some of his supposedly honorable deeds were actually horrible. With patient encouragement from Agathon, he had described excessive punishments delivered to captured soldiers, the burning of an Armenian village that posed no threat to his soldiers or the Roman Empire, and the faces of countless women and children abused, sold, or abandoned on his orders.

"Agathon anointed George's forehead, eyes, ears, mouth, chest, hands, and feet with some kind of oil."

"Now it is time for the baptism," announced Agathon. The women in the crowd turned around while two slaves took the rough blanket off Marcellus' body. Grabbing Agathon's hand, Marcellus stepped into the fountain completely naked yet, to his surprise, without embarrassment. He knelt down in the shallow, cold water.

Agathon filled a bucket. He said, "I baptize you, George, in the name of the Father..." and then poured the bucket of water over Marcellus' head. He filled the bucket again, said, "And the Son..." and poured again. He repeated the action, saying, "And the Holy Spirit. Amen."

"Amen!" the people echoed loudly.

Agathon led George out of the fountain, and Pasikrates helped him put on a new, scratchy, white robe that had been made by some slaves that very morning. Agathon anointed George's forehead, eyes, ears, mouth, chest, hands, and feet with some kind of oil. The women turned back toward the fountain when Agathon began chanting prayers again. George breathed deeply, closed his eyes, and smiled until the prayers were done. He opened his eyes when he heard Agathon begin speaking to the crowd.

"A few days ago, brothers and sisters, we prayed together at a funeral, commending the life of Synderikos to the Lord. Today, we pray together at another funeral. Marcellus was baptized unto his death and raised up as George, and we now commend his life to the Lord as well. This time, we do not picture anyone falling asleep in the Lord, but someone who is awake, who will live his life for the Lord, who will live his life in and for the Kingdom.

"What kind of work will he do? Works of love. He will love God in worship and in submission to his commandments. He will love himself by continually repenting and being cleansed of sin and by accepting more and more of God's power in his life. He will love his neighbor as he loves himself by exercising that power for the good of others. Perhaps he will perform miracles. If he does, they will be miracles like those of our Lord Jesus – acts designed to heal and re-store, not acts that call attention to himself or reveal a lust for glory. Most likely, God's power will help him do the things we all do to love our neighbor: bury the dead, protect the innocent, instruct the ignorant, forgive a wrongdoer, pray for friends and enemies alike.

These acts, just like spectacular miracles, reveal the power of God in a man.

"I have given Marcellus the name 'George.' This may seem odd. Why would an accomplished man, an esteemed and honored soldier, be given a name that means 'farmer,' a notably humble profession? But I have prayed for Marcellus — I mean, George – and I have listened to the Lord. This man, I think, will be a great farmer for the Kingdom. He will prepare ground and cultivate seeds for the Kingdom's future harvests. Let us now welcome this noble farmer George as our brother with a kiss of peace and the promise of our prayers."

Agathon lightly embraced George and kissed him once on his left cheek, once on his right cheek, then once more on his left cheek. Pasikrates did the same, and George had to wipe the mixture of his and Pasikrates' tears off his face. Then everyone in the crowd lined up to bestow the "kiss of peace" that, until that moment, George knew nothing about. He did not know how long it took to receive everyone's kiss. As he looked at each face, he felt love, and he knew that it was the power of God that Agathon had talked about. He even felt this way with those from neighboring estates whom he barely knew. He was humbled by the slaves who greeted him as "Master," especially those who were soldiers that he had captured. A few times, he was so overwhelmed by the thought of a former enemy embracing him in love that he could not look his new brother in the face.

"I still do not know what to do," George said to Agathon and Pasikrates as they enjoyed some food and wine in George's room.

Agathon replied, "I can only repeat what you have said. Your situation is dire, and you probably should not stay on this estate any longer."

"But who will protect it if I leave? Pasikrates?"

Pasikrates face betrayed his alarm. "Not I, master!"

"The better, question, George," said Agathon with quiet seriousness, "is who will protect it if you stay?"

George sighed. As he drank some more wine, he quickly ran through his options. Again, he found that none of them were good. Whether he remained on the estate or left, the dragon still won.

"Perhaps," said Pasikrates, "you need to think like a soldier, master."

"What do you mean?" asked George and Agathon at the same time.

"Well, I was thinking," began Pasikrates. As he continued to explain his ideas, George's eyes got wide.

When Pasikrates finished, George laughed. "I have been a fool. I have missed it all along. What do you think, Agathon?"

"You are right – you have been a fool. Along with me, I might add. You are the only one who can manage it."

That is true, thought George, and he suddenly remembered the words, "Protect my ships." He stood up, looked at the ceiling with outstretched arms, and said, "Thank you, Lord. I am not worthy of such a call, but I accept."

Agathon said, "Amen. I can think of no one better."

"Nor can I," added Pasikrates.

"In any case, my brothers," George said to both of them, "we will be lucky – or blessed, I should say – if we can carry out such a plan, and we have much to do if that blessing comes our way."

CHAPTER TWENTY

THE DEPARTURE

Three days later, as the sun half-appeared on the horizon, the Christians of the estate gathered in the courtyard. Agathon chanted prayers while the others from neighboring estates sang responses and hymns at the appropriate times. Only one thing was obviously different from other prayer services at the estate: George sang and prayed with his slaves and the others. Still, an onlooker would have been puzzled, for most of the people were crying, and it was clearly not a funeral service.

It was the day that George and six other Christian men would leave the estate to fight the dragon. And everyone expected that there would be no happy endings. If the men did not get killed by the dragon, they would be Christian outlaws in the Empire.

George was not ashamed to weep with the others. He did not weep for the loss of his estate. He wept for the father he loved and who was near death. He wept for the Christians around him – the "local church" as Agathon called it. In the past three days, the love and gratitude he had felt for them at his baptism had grown. Those who were his slaves still referred to him as "Master," but he felt compelled to call them "brother" or "sister," even though that usually embarrassed them. With these people, George felt a new strength and joy, even though he continued to manage the estate as usual.

Part of George also wept for the death of the Empire in his mind. The day after his baptism, he had received a letter from Cephalus. It read,

From Cephalus, a commander in the great army of Rome, to the noble Titus and the tribune Marcellus, greetings in the name of the Emperor.

I know that there are Christians on your estate, including a well-known and well-traveled liar named Lysander, also known as Agathon. The divine Emperor Diocletian, along with Caesar Galerius, desire peace, and have thus decreed that Christians be eradicated from the Empire. There can be no peace between honorable citizens of the Empire and those who defy the Empire's gods. As the humble servant of the gods and the divine Emperor Diocletian, I wish to warn you about these Christians. They may seem peaceable, but they will destroy your estate and the glorious Empire. I trust in your ability to eliminate them from your estate, and I place my soldiers at your disposal for that purpose.

Cephalus

When he showed Agathon the letter, Agathon was silent, then said, "It is properly worded, would you not say?" Amidst intense preparations to fight the dragon, this was a rare lighthearted moment.

George understood the indirect threat of Cephalus' words: If you do not eliminate these Christians, I will. He also understood why the dragon had not attacked again. Cephalus or the dragon must have decided to give George – or, in their minds, Marcellus – another chance to join them. For Cephalus, George's allegiance would be a mark of distinction that would probably lead to a promotion. The dragon would conquer one more soul and have one more estate aligned against the Christians it hated so much.

The letter also brought unexpected and unintentional benefits. It gave George time to prepare himself, his soldiers, and his estate for his departure. It also revealed that he had to include Cephalus in his plans if he wanted to protect the Christians on his estate. The more George reflected on it, the more he was grateful that such a letter had been written. Despite its dire contents, it was, he told Agathon, the blessing he was looking for. "It is definitely a gift from the Lord," was Agathon's reply.

The morning prayer service was nearly over. Agathon called George and the other six soldiers to him. The people gathered around them.

"We all know what these men have agreed to attempt," said Agathon to the crowd around George, "and so we honor them as Christians should honor people: with prayer and with water from George's baptism."

Agathon stretched his arms out and prayed so that everyone could hear him: "Heavenly Father, our tower of strength, be with these men as they go to accomplish their task. Grant them courage, strength, faithfulness, and love as they face this enemy of mankind. Amen."

"Amen," came the reply.

Agathon grabbed a vial of water, said a short prayer, and sprinkled water on George's head, saying, "Bless the servant of God George, in the name of the Father and the Son and the Holy Spirit." He then did the same for the others.

After the final prayer and many more tears and embraces, George made a last inspection of the horses and equipment for his attack. He regretted that he only had four horses besides Kopto, but he knew that any attempt to get more would become known to Cephalus and the dragon and certainly prompt another attack. Five horses for seven men will have to suffice, he thought.

He realized that he should be thankful for the four that he had, even if it meant being thankful for the bandits who attacked him. In the twenty-one days that these horses had been in Titus' stables, they had ceased to look like bedraggled pack-horses and had begun to act like war horses. They were clearly inspired by the proud bearing and work-loving Kopto. When Kopto exercised, they strove to keep up with him. When Kopto bent to George's command, they began to pay attention to their own riders.

Each horse was saddled, and George counted the spears, swords, and shields attached to each saddle. He looked at the scarce provisions and again resisted the urge to pack more food. He went over the miscellaneous equipment: a hammer, some rope, a flint, a shovel, and a few other things. He fought the urge to find places for more gear.

The six men blessed by Agathon along with George walked to the horses. George noticed their determined expressions and knew that they were ready. All six were foreign soldiers whom George had captured in a raid or a battle. Like the other slaves, they were embarrassed when George called them "brothers," but he also saw their love for him and their faith rekindled by his address. All had eagerly volunteered to be a part of this attack. Two of them, George knew, were leaving wives and children behind – and they knew that they would probably never come back.

"Take your places, brothers," George ordered. As they moved, George recalled their Christian names. Elias and Ionas, he thought, as two former Sassanid soldiers walked over to one of the brown horses. Micah, he remembered, as another Sassanid grabbed the reins of the other brown horse. When two Persians took their place by the grey horse, he recalled that they were Lucas and Dionysius. George remembered the last man with ease, for he was an Armenian who had been a Christian – and therefore Petrus – before being captured. He watched with pleasure as Petrus rechecked the saddle and equipment on the white horse that resembled Kopto.

"Go in peace, George."

George turned and faced Agathon and Pasikrates.

"Go in peace," Agathon said again, and George bowed as Agathon laid his right hand on George's head and then embraced him. George felt tears return to his eyes.

"Thank you" was all he could think to say.

Agathon moved past George to bless and bid farewell to the others. Pasikrates moved forward, his cheeks wet with tears. To stop himself from sobbing, George focused on matters relating to the estate.

"You have the letters and the will in a safe place?" George asked.

"Yes, my master."

"Who are they for?"

"One is for Demetrios, detailing Cephalus' activities with bandits and explaining your decision to become a Christian and" – Pasikrates held back a sob and took a deep breath – "and an outlaw."

"And the other letter?"

"The other is for your father in case he wakes up."

George had to hold down his tears when his father was mentioned. He continued: "You know where to bury my father?"

"Yes, my master."

"And you know the terms of the will?"

Pasikrates hesitated, then said "yes" reluctantly. Before George could say anything else, Pasikrates blurted out, "But I cannot do it! I cannot take it and manage it! How will I defend anyone?"

"If the dragon kills me, then it makes no difference who is in charge of the estate. You must lead as many people as you can to safety. If I live, then everyone here knows the will. They know that they will be free and that you will be the new owner. They will listen to you like they always do. Agathon will be here to help you every once in a while."

"I still cannot do it! I am afraid!"

George gripped Pasikrates' shoulder and looked into his eyes. This is no different, he thought, from helping a frightened young soldier before battle. "Pasikrates – no, Mercurius, my Christian brother – this is not about your freedom or the wealth of the estate. Think about the people here, about the Kingdom that Agathon talks about – the one now and the one to come. You must – we must – do this for the Kingdom."

Pasikrates bowed his head and nodded, weeping. George embraced him and stopped holding back his own tears.

Then George and the six men rode off to fight the dragon.

* * *

George took an indirect route to the cave in hopes that no one would see them and be able to warn the dragon. Whatever the dragon expected, George knew, it was not an attack from seven men on five horses in the middle of the day. He did not want to give up this element of surprise which was, he was certain, one of the few advantages he had. So instead of traveling easily through Lucius' estate, George led the others, sometimes on foot and always slowly, through the brush, woods, and overgrown grasses on the edge of Lucius' estate. No one complained. They are true soldiers, George thought with delight as he delivered a silent prayer of thanks to God.

The ride proved uneventful. They saw no one. After they were well beyond the border of Lucius' estate, they rode openly through the increasingly barren landscape. As George had hoped, the day was hot and dry. Rain, he knew, almost always made a soldier's work harder.

As George had expected, the mood of the men shifted as they traveled. No words were exchanged, but their faces became more tense as the landscape became blacker and more lifeless. George did not fault them for this. He knew the dread caused by an impending encounter with the dragon.

As they came to the top of the cliff overlooking the dragon's cave, George called a halt. The men dismounted silently, drank some water, and ate some bread. George called them together.

"I will be brief, brothers. In a moment, I will crawl to the edge of the cliff to see if the dragon is outside its cave. But first, a question

I have asked before: Are you here freely? For you are free men now. Do not fear any dishonor if you wish to return and help Pasikrates and Agathon."

All six men nodded without taking their eyes off George. Only Ionas spoke. "We follow you, brother George, because you are leading us against an enemy of our true leader, the Lord Jesus Christ."

George's heart swelled with gratitude. "Good, brothers, good. You are willing, and I know that courage does not come from unwilling soldiers. And we will need courage. You have never faced an enemy like this, and you have never fought with so little promise for a reward. The dragon has no gold, silver, or land. This fight is, indeed, only for the Lord and his Kingdom. If we defeat this beast, we only win the label of outlaws in the Empire. And it is almost certain that some of us or all of us will not live to see the sun rise tomorrow. But I am not afraid to fall asleep in the Lord, and I know that you are not either. So let us fight bravely, and let us fight with intelligence. This dragon is unlike any other creature you have seen, but it is still a creature. Aim for any exposed skin, its eyes, under its scales, and most of all where the wings join the body. We are doomed if it flies to attack us or to tell Cephalus about us. Now, it is time to be soldiers again, brothers. We dare not sing, so let us pray silently together before we descend."

They all bowed their heads. George could only think of a simple prayer: Lord, have mercy on us and grant us victory over the enemy. When he looked up, the others were looking at him, waiting for him to begin.

George turned toward the edge of the cliff and dropped to his knees. He quickly crawled to the edge. He desperately hoped to see the dragon alone. He did not want to coax it out of its cave, and he knew that a fight would be truly hopeless if some of Cephalus' soldiers were there.

When he was able to peer over the edge of the cliff, he saw the dragon well away from its cave. There were no signs of any soldiers nearby. But he saw something else, and he had to cover his mouth to squelch the cry that came out.

In front of the motionless dragon, in a limply hanging, brightly colored robe, was Regina. She stood, arms outstretched and head pointing toward the sky, saying something. Then she dropped to her knees and bowed her head while keeping her arms outstretched. The dragon flicked its tail. At that moment, George knew what was happening. Regina was offering herself to the dragon, and the dragon was about to accept.

CHAPTER TWENTY-ONE

THE BATTLE

George scrambled back and hurriedly climbed onto Kopto.

"Now, men, now! Regina is with the dragon! Try to keep the dragon away from her! Now! As fast as you can!"

George turned Kopto and spurred him along the path heading to the bottom of the cliff. As Kopto raced down the path, George did not look back to see if the others were close to him. A horse less sure-footed than Kopto would have thrown its rider at Kopto's speed.

When George reached the plain, he spurred Kopto again and rushed to ride between Regina and the dragon. The dragon noticed him and flicked its tail. Regina opened her eyes and stood up. As George got closer, the dragon did not move or seem to prepare for any kind of attack. A foolish beast, thought George. Even now it thinks that I will submit to it.

George and Kopto stopped between Regina and the dragon.

"Marcellus, have you – " Regina began to ask before George waved her silent.

The dragon stared at George. This time, George saw hatred and a bottomless appetite in its red eyes. Out of the corner of his own eyes, he saw Dionysius and Lucas, riding together, making a broad sweep behind the dragon. He also saw Petrus and Micah racing toward him on their horses.

So far, thought George, this is perfect. The dragon is so focused on me that my soldiers are getting in position.

"Hello, Marcellus," said the dragon with its smooth voice.

Regina, who had been watching the other men, turned to the dragon and yelled, "He is here to kill you!"

The dragon finally looked around. George saw his chance, grabbed his loosened spear, and lunged, aiming for the dragon's eye. Regina screamed. The dragon turned back to George, and the spear made a shallow cut through its snout. The dragon bellowed in pain and filled the air around George with a foul stench.

The dragon wildly lunged and snapped at George. Kopto reared up and hit the dragon on its fresh cut with a hoof. The dragon bellowed again. The doubling of the stench made George retch and nearly lose his grip on Kopto.

The dragon will attack me while I am vulnerable, flashed through George's mind. Then he heard another ear-splitting bellow. He looked up and saw Petrus yanking back a spear that had penetrated under the scales. The dragon jerked its tail, causing Petrus' white horse to rear up. As Petrus fell to the ground, the dragon whirled around. In one movement, it lunged and sunk its teeth into his neck. After giving out a short cry, Petrus went limp.

Enraged, George threw his spear. As it bounced uselessly off the dragon's back, Dionysius rode by and slashed the dragon's wing. The dragon bellowed again, and Dionysius grabbed the reins of Petrus' horse and raced away. George turned Kopto around and moved away from the dragon while he had the chance. The dragon started to pursue him but was stopped as it tried to extend its injured wing.

George felt a momentary rush of victory. It cannot fly, he thought, so it will have to fight us.

The dragon looked around and seemed to quickly assess its situation. Then it turned and charged toward its cave. In front of the cave was Lucas, on foot and holding his spear and shield. When the dragon was near Lucas, it stopped. It walked forward slowly, belching flames. Lucas stood still, and the angry dragon's fire became more intense. As the flames licked the shield, Lucas remained still.

Out of the corner of his eye, George saw a brown horse race by on his right. It is Micah, he thought. He is taking advantage of Lucas' distraction.

Two things happened at nearly the same time. Lucas, with flames encircling his shield, yelled out a war cry and charged the dragon. He raised his spear so that it and his right hand were enveloped in flames. He thrust the spear forward, and it caught the dragon in its eye. Before the dragon could bellow, Micah rode in and plunged his spear where the dragon's broken wing met its body. George saw at least one-quarter of the spear disappear into the dragon.

The sound from the dragon that followed made George cover his ears. He saw it roll over while Micah dashed away to safety. When its soft underbelly appeared, George saw another chance. He readied his sword and was about to spur Kopto when he felt a sharp blow on his head and lost consciousness.

As soon as he opened his eyes, George knew that little time had passed. He was lying on the ground with his sword half on his chest, Kopto was still close to him, and the dragon was still bellowing. Suddenly, a large rock appeared above his head. He quickly twisted his body and felt the rock land on his back, temporarily knocking out his breath. When he turned over again, Regina was standing above him, her face full of rage.

"You deserve to die, you traitor!" she screamed. "I will offer you to the dragon first!"

As Regina started picking up the rock that had just come off his back, George tried to stand up. His spinning head and lack of breath made him fall down again before he was on his knees.

Expecting to be hit with the rock, George instead saw a brown blur and heard Regina scream in anguish. After taking in a deep breath, he managed to get to his feet. In front of him was Elias on his brown horse. On the other side of Elias was Regina.

"Do not hurt her!" he yelled. The exertion it took to yell caused his head to spin again. He fell to his knees.

"Master Marcellus! I mean, Master George! Quick!" said a voice he thought belonged to Elias.

George looked up and saw nothing but a bare expanse.

"The other way!" yelled the same voice.

He turned around on his knees and saw the dragon advancing toward him. Beyond the dragon, Micah was off his horse, hovering over an unmoving Lucas. Elias was to his right, shielding him from a hysterical Regina.

"Master, take my spear!" shouted Elias, throwing it to him. Somehow, he managed to catch it.

Suddenly, Kopto was in front of him. George found the strength to stand up with the spear in his hand. The dragon continued to advance, its head turned in one direction so that it could see George with its unharmed eye.

The dragon abruptly broke into a run and then lunged at Kopto. Kopto reared up and again hit the dragon's snout with his hoof, but the dragon quickly toppled him and began to ferociously tear the horse to pieces.

George suddenly felt strong again and was about to charge the dragon when Dionysius rode in front of him, leading Petrus' white horse.

"Grab the reins! Get on! Quickly!"

Leaving George holding the white horse's reins, Dionysius charged the dragon, spear in hand. George struggled against the urge to follow Dionysius on foots and climbed onto the horse. He saw the dragon turn its good eye toward Dionysius. Before George could shout, the dragon flicked its tail so that it swept under the hoofs of Dionysius' horse. Dionysius threw his spear before his horse tumbled, but, like George's, it bounced harmlessly off the dragon's flank. Dionysius and his horse fell to the ground. As the dragon advanced, the horse reared up. The dragon waited until the horse was on all fours again to lunge. The horse bolted quickly enough to escape, but the dragon then pounced on a motionless Dionysius.

By this time, George was sturdily on the white horse. He grabbed the spear that Elias had thrown him and charged the dragon. The dragon looked up and turned its head toward Micah, who had re-mounted his horse and was proceeding cautiously toward it. Then,

George saw the trap. Elias swooped in on the dragon's blind side, jumped down, and plunged his sword under the dragon's unharmed wing. As the dragon bellowed forth a ball of flame and turned toward Elias, Micah charged forward and drove his spear where he had driven it before. This time, only half of it was visible by the time he was done.

The dragon roared again and rolled backward toward Micah. Elias quickly jumped off his horse and drove his sword into the exposed underbelly, causing the dragon to roar again. He plunged the sword in again, and the dragon jerked and knocked him over. If he had not scrambled away immediately, he would have been pinned under the dragon's writhing body.

By this time, George was near the dragon. Micah was getting ready to dismount with his sword. Before George could drive his own spear into the dragon, he saw Regina running toward the dragon. He stopped his horse.

"Micah, get out of there!" he yelled, pointing at Regina. "Stop her!"

Micah sheathed his sword and rode toward Regina. Regina began screaming as Micah got near to her.

George turned back to the dragon with his spear ready. The dragon's tail twitched as it tried and failed to right its body. George looked for the best place to strike before moving closer. He knew that he still had to be cautious. The dragon, like a panicking man, was unpredictable.

When George started to move closer, the dragon managed to aim its good eye at him.

"Marcellus," it croaked, "it is still not too late."

"My name is George."

"No, Marcellus, you are not one of them."

George was over the dragon. "My name is George," he repeated.

The dragon, in a flash, mustered its strength and lunged upward toward George, jaws open. George's horse reared up. As it came down, George thrust his spear between the dragon's teeth. The force of his strength and the horse's weight drove the spear through the dragon's head and out the back side of its neck. The dragon's body went limp and thudded to the ground.

Regina screamed. When George turned to look at her, she had collapsed into Micah's arms.

George smelled the dragon's body and foul breath and again retched. Then he straightened himself on the white horse, took a shallow breath, and wiped his mouth in grim satisfaction.

CHAPTER TWENTY-TWO

AFTER THE BATTLE

Suddenly, a wave of exhaustion passed through George's body. He fell forward on to the white horse's neck. He would have fallen off if Elias had not scrambled to hold him on.

George felt a small measure of strength return. "Help me down," he said hoarsely to Elias.

Slowly, he pulled his leg over the horse while holding its neck. Elias pushed upward on the other leg until George nodded. Then Elias gently let George's body down and steadied him until he nodded again.

George looked around. Ionas was racing toward him on foot, and Micah was setting the unconscious Regina down. The bodies of Lucas, Petrus, and Dionysius lay haphazardly on the ground. Kopto's shining white hide was mangled and blotched with dark stains. A pool of blood was collecting under the dragon's head. He took a deep breath, smelled the dragon again, and gripped Elias to steady himself.

"Let us..." George began, but found it too difficult to say anything else. Elias understood. Leaning on each other, George and Elias walked toward the oncoming Ionas.

* * *

"Here's some water, master."

"Do we have plenty?"

"Probably."

George poured water on his head and wiped his face clean. Then he drank until the water skin was empty. When he looked up, he saw Micah and Elias do the same, with Ionas providing the water. He felt a surge of pride. The dragon was dead, and there was hope for the Christian community at his father's estate. But he also recalled the faces of Lucas, Petrus, and Dionysius. When he turned and saw the lifeless, bloodied Kopto, he felt hot anger in his face. And Cephalus is still alive, he thought, so the estate is not safe.

George closed his eyes. "Think like a soldier," he said softly to himself. The first person to come to mind was Ionas, who was gathering the water skins.

George said commandingly, "Ionas, there was no dishonor in keeping your post. With you there, the dragon did not think to escape up the hill."

"I know, master."

"You will have other chances to prove your valor, I am sure."

Ionas smiled, but not the smile of a young soldier getting much-needed encouragement. "Thank you, master. I will prove my valor if I need to. But I have no need for honor. I received all the honor I would ever need when I was baptized, and the honor keeps flowing to me when I pray and worship. I only desire to serve the Kingdom now, whether that means guarding an escape route, plowing a field, or providing water for my brothers."

George was startled. Then he remembered everything he had learned since he had arrived at his father's estate. He realized that, despite his baptism, he was still not prone to think like a Christian. The gentle tone of Ionas' words prevented any shame, though, so he was able to quickly turn his mind back to this situation.

"Well-spoken, Ionas. A good reminder for a new Christian like me. Now, I am sorry to say this, brothers, but we cannot rest much more. When Cephalus gets news of the dragon, he will probably hunt us down or begin raiding the estate again. We have three or four days of provisions, right?"

Ionas nodded. "If we can find more water," he added.

"There are many sources of water nearby, so that is not a worry." George looked up at the sky. "We have just enough time to finish our work here, and we have four horses for four men. Ionas and Micah, stay here and bury the bodies of our brothers. We will pray beside their graves tonight. Use the rope and pull Kopto and the beast into the cave. The longer they are out of view, the longer it will be before anyone knows about the dragon's death. Elias and I should return before sunset. If you cannot move the dragon with two horses, we will try in the morning with four."

He turned to Elias. "You and I will bring Regina back to her father. Let us drink and eat something quickly so that we do not collapse on the way."

* * *

The ride to Lucius' estate was slow and silent. At first, George filled the time thinking about strategy for possible confrontations with Cephalus. At some point, however, it occurred to him that he should spend the time praying. There will be plenty of time for strategy in the next few days, he thought.

So, as the tired horses plodded and as he continually shifted to prevent the unconscious Regina from falling, George prayed. He prayed for Agathon, Pasikrates (or Mercurius, he thought to himself), and the Christians on the estate. He prayed for Ionas and Micah, thinking of the disagreeable work of burying their comrades and brothers. He did not know what to pray concerning Lucas, Petrus, and Dionysius, so he simply asked the Lord to have mercy on them. He remembered Jesus' words about enemies, and proceeded, despite the anger in his mind, to pray for Lucius, Cephalus, Regina, Diocletian, Galerius, and all of the other enemies of Christianity that he could think of.

Not long after he and Elias reached the edge of Lucius' estate, they were spotted by two slaves who were herding sheep. One of the slaves walked over to greet them, but grew pale when he recognized Regina and George.

George looked at the slave squarely. "Go and tell your master what you have seen."

The slave turned and sprinted away.

George looked at Elias. "We will have to be more careful now."

Elias patted his sword in acknowledgment.

* * *

Not long before he expected to see Lucius' villa, George saw three horses approaching. As they came closer, George recognized Lucius and saw that the other men carried swords.

"Do not worry, Elias. None of Lucius' slaves are former soldiers. They will not know how to use horses or swords."

"One of them might," replied Elias. "The man on the left is Melchior, I think."

George recognized him immediately. The slave who betrayed me, he thought. He checked to make sure that his sword and spear could be drawn easily.

Lucius called a halt when he was within speaking distance of George and Elias. George scanned the faces of the other men, looking for signs of nervousness or defiance. They seemed tense, but none seemed ready to charge. They kept their hands on the reins of their horses. Lucius does not want a confrontation any more than I do, he thought.

"Not long before he expected to see Lucius' villa, George saw three horses approaching."

"What have you done with her, Marcellus?" shouted Lucius.

"My name is George."

Lucius snorted in contempt. "Answer me, Marcellus!"

"Do you know that you have a traitor in your midst?" George replied.

Lucius looked at Melchior, then barked back, "You mean a man who worships the gods and loves the Empire? Yes, I will gladly house that sort of traitor."

Melchior sneered, and George decided not to answer. After a long silence, Lucius shouted again, "What have you done with her?"

"I have done nothing but save her – and not just me, but Elias here, too, and five others. Three of them paid with their lives to rescue her."

"Your pitiful slaves are of no interest to me."

"But your daughter is, and she is now safe."

"Not safe from you."

"Safe from the dragon and herself. We rescued her from the dragon."

"She worships the dragon. It would not hurt her."

"Even the dragon could not resist Regina offering herself. She would be in the dragon's belly right now if I – if we – had not rescued her."

George thought he saw Lucius turn pale. "I do not believe you," said Lucius, although not as loudly.

"Believe what you will, my friend. She is here, and she is safe."

"Do not call me friend, blaspheming Christian!"

"I am a Christian, and I would be your friend."

"I do not want the friendship of a traitorous Christian. And I want my daughter back!"

George paused to let Lucius' anger recede. Then he spoke. "Of course. Now back yourself and your men up. When you are a safe distance away, Elias will dismount and ease Regina to the ground. Then he and I will ride away. Do not try anything rash, Lucius. I am a Christian, but I am a soldier as well. I will defend myself, Elias, and Regina. We come here in peace and wish to leave in peace."

Without acknowledging George, Lucius and the two men turned and rode away for a short distance, then stopped and turned to face George and Elias again.

George whispered to the still unconscious woman, "Good-bye, Regina. I am sorry I caused you pain. I will pray for you."

Elias did as George said he would. As the two of them rode toward the dragon's cave, George looked back more than once. To his relief, Lucius' men did not pursue him.

CHAPTER TWENTY-THREE

A LETTER

Four months later, George wrote Pasikrates this letter:

From George, also known as Marcellus, former soldier of the Roman Empire and now a slave of Jesus Christ, to Mercurius, also known as Pasikrates, my former slave and now a brother in Christ. Greetings in the name of the Lord.

I used to presume that only a slave would put ink on parchment. Now I repent of such folly. Repentance cannot steady my unpracticed hand, however. You, no longer my slave but always Christ's slave, will have to endure my handwriting with patience.

It is fitting that I write this while sitting in a slave's quarters. For now I am, like you, a slave of Christ, and

*stations of lowliness must now be seen as stations of glory. I
am on Caius Gallus' estate. He is sympathetic to Christians
and may even become one. He was surprised that I had
become a Christian and left my estate, but when I told him
about the dragon, he only nodded gravely. He, too, knows
that the greatness of Rome is disappearing.*

*This letter must bear as much bad news as my previous letter.
Ionas is ill, and by the time you receive this letter, he will be
asleep in the Lord unless the miracle we pray for comes to
pass. With his death, the party of seven that left the estate
will be a party of three. And with Galerius continuing his
murderous campaign against Christians, that number may
grow smaller still. We have heard that he has spies in many
estates, most of them slaves looking to earn their freedom.
That is why we have moved so much. I do not wish to be
captured, and I do not want our hosts to feel any of Galerius'
wrath.*

*In my last letter, I told you how we killed the dragon and
saved Regina. I sent that letter in a hurry, having just heard
news of soldiers in the area. Now I must finish the story, and
I will start with some good news: your estate is safe for now,
for Cephalus is dead.*

*It was not difficult to avoid the three soldiers that Cephalus
sent to consult with the dragon, for as soon as they discovered
that the dragon was dead, they bolted back to their camp.
Actually, only two of the three returned. The other emerged
from the dragon's cave, laughing and flailing his arms. When
the other two came near him, he slashed at them wildly with*

a knife, still laughing. He didn't seem to notice when they rode off without him, taking his horse.

We followed the two soldiers at some distance, but I do not think that we needed to be careful. They were either poorly trained or men who were panicking. They never looked to see if they were being followed or if there was any danger nearby. They barely ate or slept. While following their path, we came upon one of their horses, on the ground, nearly dead from exhaustion. But they never slowed their pace for the other horses. When we arrived at the camp, everything was burning, and no one could be found alive. Cephalus had been beaten severely, and a few other soldiers lay near him, probably killed because they tried to defend him. I thought, "Cephalus received a just reward," but I should have thought, "May God have mercy on his soul."

With Cephalus gone and his soldiers scattered, you should be safe on the estate for a short while. You must remain vigilant, however. Diocletian and Galerius will not succeed in destroying our faith, but many Christians will die at their hands before they fail. Be hospitable to strangers, but beware of spies. Know that Galerius will replace Cephalus with a commander twice as full of hate and guile. Do not forget the plans for leaving the estate. You must flee while danger is far off. Remember Agathon's words: none should be afraid of martyrdom, but none should seek it.

Your letter brought many blessings. I gloried that Regina was safe and recovering. How I wish I knew more! She and Lucius are probably still full of rage. We have continued to pray for them. *Your tender regard for me makes me weep, as does your tender remembrance of my father. Knowing that you will pray by my father's grave comforts me, but I weep more when I think that I may never pray there. May God have mercy on his noble soul.*

Why is it, my brother, that I rarely wept before I became a slave of Christ? Was I so blind to my own sinful heart, the hearts of others, and even the beauty of this world? Yes, yes, and yes again, in my soldierly way. I wince when I remember that I was willing to lose my soul for the whole Roman world.

I hope, my dear brother, that this answers your concern about my faith. I would like to say that I have steadfastly kept my faith in the Lord, but it feels more like he is steadfastly keeping faith in me. A slave on Caius Gallus' estate had a copy of one of the Apostle's letters. There was much I did not understand, but I will never forget these words: "neither death nor life, neither angels nor demons, neither the present nor the future, nor any powers, neither height nor depth, nor anything else in all creation, will be able to separate us from the love of God that is in Christ Jesus our Lord."

We will leave this estate soon. We have strengthened and been strengthened by the Christians here. Perhaps we will head north to the estate of Antonius. I have heard that the Christians there worship freely. I have also heard that Antonius is in league with Galerius. Either way, I go to cultivate for the Lord, for he has made me a farmer. I will not see the fruits of my labor, but there will be fruits, for the Lord is planting, cultivating, and harvesting.

I say farewell, knowing that my life is in danger whether I am in the safety of a slave's quarters or hiding on the outskirts of Antonius' estate. Do not weep, my dear brother, but pray that the Lord will use this farmer for the glory of his kingdom. I weep as I write this. Know that we pray for you and those on your estate. Give my greetings to Agathon when he arrives.

CHAPTER TWENTY-FOUR

THE LAST FOUR YEARS

George, Elias, and Micah devoted the next four years to disrupting networks of Roman spies and bringing much-needed news and supplies to Christians around Galatia. They arrived at some estates as heroes, receiving food and rest. They hid on the edges of other estates, fearful of discovery and betrayal.

Elias eventually fell prey to illness and was buried at the edge of an obscure field. Micah was captured a short while later and executed as an escaped slave. George was captured soon after and executed as a traitor.

The Christian communities that George and his companions protected thrived after Galerius died and the persecution of Christians ended. These communities forgot Micah, Elias, Ionas, Dionysius, Petrus, Lucas, Mercurius, and Agathon, but they remembered the courageous and faithful leader who slew a dragon and protected Christians, the great saint and martyr George.

THE END

ACKNOWLEDGEMENTS

Many thanks to my family and friends for believing that this story should be told. Thanks also to all my preliminary readers, children and adults: your comments made this story better. Special thanks to Paul and Cindy Karos for their steadfast faith in God and their exceptional generosity.

More praise for *St. George and the Dragon*...

"Michael Lotti weaves history, faith and fantasy into a seamless and powerful whole. This compelling, full-fledged work of historical and spiritual fiction captures our hearts and imaginations and challenges us to face and conquer the dragons we face every day."

— Fr. Richard René, Author of the Mysterion Series

"This rendition of the tale of St. George is sure to inspire young readers. Michael Lotti has crafted a wonderful tale about the dragon-slayer within the context of the late Roman Empire, beautifully capturing the tension between the city of man and the city of God."

— Michael Adkins, Academic Dean of St. Agnes School, St. Paul, Minnesota

"This book was irresistible and delightful. It powerfully shows the distinction between choosing the Christian good that masks itself in humility and evil that appears too intriguing and powerful to resist."

— Fr. Benjamin Tucci, Youth Director and Associate Pastor, St. Mary's Cathedral, Minneapolis, Minnesota

CPSIA information can be obtained
at www.ICGtesting.com
Printed in the USA
LVHW04s1823200818
586748LV00006B/210/P